CP 007

CW00803259

J. Cl

RF

LARGE PRINT

Awarded for excellence in public service
Dumfries and Galloway
Libraries, Information and Archives

THE TREASURE WITHIN

THE TREASURE WITHIN

Catherine Cross

Chivers Press
Bath, England

•

Thorndike Press
Waterville, Maine USA

This Large Print edition is published by Chivers Press, England, and by Thorndike Press, USA.

Published in 2003 in the U.K. by arrangement with the author.

Published in 2003 in the U.S. by arrangement with Mary Cross.

U.K. Hardcover ISBN 0–7540–8927–4 (Chivers Large Print)
U.S. Softcover   ISBN 0–7862–5139–5 (Nightingale Series)

The text of this Large Print edition is unabridged.
Other aspects of the book may vary from the original edition.

Set in 16 pt. New Times Roman.

Printed in Great Britain on acid-free paper.

British Library Cataloguing in Publication Data available

Library of Congress Cataloging-in-Publication Data

Cross, Catherine, 1945–
     The treasure within / by Catherine Cross.
          p.   cm.
     ISBN 0–7862–5139–5 (lg. print : sc : alk. paper)
     1. Large type books. I. Title.
PR6053.R598T74 2003
823'.92—dc21   2002075695

CHAPTER ONE

A movement through the trees caught Rosalind's attention as she looked up from the piece of embroidery she had been restoring. Having worked on the antique dining chair for most of the day, Ros needed a change of focus, so she walked to the window and concentrated on the parkland that stretched into the distance. Today a small herd of Highland cattle was grazing contentedly on the lush spring grass, a few calves frisking at their mother's feet, enjoying the first really warm day of the year.

A car was making its way slowly up the long drive towards the house.

'Now who can this be?' she mused.

A frown marred Rosalind's face and she tugged at her lower lip with small, even teeth. Who could be coming up to the house today? Obviously no-one on estate business, as they usually went up the back roads to the farm and the estate manager's office. Perhaps someone had lost their way and thought the drive was, in fact, a small road. It had happened before.

The afternoon sun streamed in through diamond-paned lattice windows, picking up the detailing of the linen-fold panelling and bouncing off the oak floor which had been polished only that morning by Mrs Barnes, the housekeeper. A half-burned log fell into the fire, breaking the silence in the room, and a small brown kitten who had been asleep on a rug in front of it woke up and stretched.

The sound also woke Mrs Barnes, who had brought her knitting with her after lunch to keep Rosalind company, and had promptly nodded off. Rosalind smiled affectionately.

'What's that then, my dear?' Mrs Barnes asked, pulling her plump body out of the fireside chair and coming to stand at the window with Ros.

'Someone coming up through the park, Mrs B. Look, there.'

Ros pointed into the middle distance. The drive, meandering as it did through the parkland, was almost half a mile long from main road to house, and the two women had plenty of time to observe the car's progress. Sometimes obscured by large rhododendron bushes lining parts of the drive, the car came closer, almost stopping once or twice as if the driver appeared intent on viewing the house before he or she reached it.

'No, it can't be! Can it?' Rosalind said.

A feeling of apprehension stole through her and squeezed at her heart.

'Do you think it's who I think it is?' Mrs Barnes said.

'Tom's nephew?' Rosalind said. 'He's got to come some time,' she said. 'After all, Tom did leave the estate to him.'

Mrs Barnes sighed.

'And all his money, too, if that solicitor knew what he was talking about.'

Rosalind turned to look at her.

'Tom never spoke to me about his nephew. You were with him for years, Mrs B. Do you know him?'

'No,' the housekeeper replied angrily. 'I don't. Never heard of him. But what sort of man would refuse to visit an uncle like Mr Tom? He was such a lovely gentleman.'

Rosalind could only shake her head in sympathy.

'I've no idea.'

'Well, I'd better go and see who it is, anyway,' Mrs Barnes said, her sensible lace-up shoes hardly making a sound as she crossed the oak floor on her way out.

Rosalind turned back to the window. Intuition told her who the new arrival was and, if she needed confirmation, she had it now as a man walked towards the narrow bridge that spanned the moat. Feelings of anger and disgust welled up in her as she watched his progress over the bridge. He was tall, like his uncle, she noticed with dark hair, thick and straight, same determined set to the jaw. The sensual mouth, obviously a family trait, had smiled happily upwards in the uncle. In the nephew it was straight and uncompromising. So this is the new owner, Ros thought, the nephew to whom Tom left his millions. The

3

person. Rosalind knew, who had not even bothered to attend the old man's funeral.

As he continued towards the massive, oak front door, Rosalind moved closer to the window and, gripping the stone mullion, leaned forward to get a better look. He must have sensed her presence. He stopped and looked up to her first-floor window and stared straight at her, brown eyes cold and unyielding in a tanned face. She gasped and shrank back from the window, an embarrassing flush colouring her normally creamy complexion at being caught spying on him. She ran a hand shakily through her hair and tried to pull herself together.

Why should I be bothered what he thinks about me? I'll be finished here in another few weeks and then all this will be just another completed commission.

Rosalind would be really sorry to leave the house she had come to love, but she sensed that having to complete her work under the watchful scrutiny of this man would be almost impossible. She was amazed at the intensity of her feeling towards the stranger. She knew it was totally illogical, but whenever had logic governed the most important decisions in her life?

The house was still in mourning, but Tom Bradshaw would never have wanted anyone to be unhappy on his account. He had been such a wonderful, old man, full of fun and ideas and extremely good company. Rosalind missed him dreadfully, despite only knowing him for a few months. He might have been her employer, and a temporary one at that, but he had become a real friend.

She paced the room, pushing her hands into the pockets of her trousers. A silk shirt and a cream sweater embroidered with roses in varying shades of pink completed the outfit, making her look soft and feminine, but Rosalind didn't feel either soft or feminine at the moment. She felt angry at the way this man had treated his uncle.

She wondered whether or not to go downstairs and meet him, but couldn't bring herself to do it. Better to leave it to Mrs Barnes who was marvellous at smoothing over difficult situations. And anyway, why should she look as if she'd nothing better to do with her time than pander to him?

If he wants to speak to me I am sure I will be summoned to his presence in due course, she thought.

She stopped pacing and picked up the kitten who had been following her up and down the room on rather wobbly legs.

'Poor sweetheart. I wonder what will happen to you now. I don't suppose he will want you, will he?' she said, cuddling the kitten and walking back towards the window.

'You don't suppose who will want it?' a cold voice said, edged with steel.

5

Rosalind spun round. The stranger was silhouetted in the doorway with Mrs Barnes hovering in the background rather out of breath, her face flushed. At a disadvantage yet again, Ros fumed. The darned man had only arrived on the scene less than five minutes ago and yet he had made her appear foolish twice already. Why hadn't she heard them come along the Long Gallery? How did he get here so quickly? She had planned to be sitting down, needlework in hand, looking totally composed when he walked in, not wandering up and down the room prattling on to the kitten about him.

'Oh, Rosalind, this is—'

Mrs Barnes' words died on her lips as the stranger held up his hand, silencing her.

'I'm still waiting for an answer,' he ground out. 'Who wouldn't want it?'

Ros drew herself up to her full five feet nine inches and, in what she hoped was a controlled voice, said, 'And who, exactly, are you?'

She felt the hairs beginning to rise on the back of her neck. Whoever was responsible for his education had forgotten the lesson in manners, she thought.

The kitten, picking up the anger emanating from her started to struggle. Rosalind lowered it gently to the floor, breaking eye contact with the man in an effort to give herself more time to prepare for the battle she felt was imminent. Cross she might be, but she wasn't

6

going to say anything more until he either apologised or found some of those manners.

'The name's Carlisle.'

He moved farther into the room, Mrs Barnes following him. There it was then, positive proof. Ros had never felt so hostile to someone in her life. Not that she was hostile to him on her own account, she reminded herself, just for what he had done, or rather, not done, for Tom.

She had been at Farthings for over four months now and not once had he been to see Tom, not even when Tom had the stroke that finally killed him. And at the funeral, attended by so many of the old man's friends and acquaintances, where was he? Nowhere to be seen.

Well, Ros thought, if he thinks he's in for an easy ride, walking in and taking over, he's got another think coming.

'So? Is the name supposed to mean something to me?' she lied.

'I'm Tom Bradshaw's nephew and the new owner of this estate.'

Well, he didn't have to be so smug about it, did he?

'Oh, really? I didn't know he had any relatives still alive,' she drawled.

She heard Mrs Barnes' gasp of amazement. Perhaps that was pushing it a bit far, Ros thought, but he deserved it.

His eyes glittered angrily at her.

7

'And you are?'

'Rosalind Greenway,' Ros said, lifting her chin and staring straight back.

'I thought as much,' he replied icily.

The kitten chose that moment to launch itself at the new owner's legs, latching its claws firmly into what looked, to Ros, like very expensive cord. It hung on, mewing plaintively. A small smile threatened to escape from her, but died when she saw his white face and closed eyes. Oh, dear, she thought, he doesn't like cats.

Mrs Barnes ran forward, tut-tutting as she went.

'You naughty boy!' she exclaimed.

She freed the cat from the cord trousers, put him outside the door and shut it firmly behind the little animal. Rosalind sighed. There was nothing a man could do if he was afraid of cats, she thought, her naturally generous nature coming to the fore. She could understand fear. Wasn't she afraid of spiders? She shuddered at the thought.

'Perhaps a pot of tea might be in order, Mrs Barnes,' she said, thinking it might restore his equilibrium, although she couldn't think for the life of her why she should be helping to put him at ease.

Mrs Barnes looked at the man, who nodded imperceptibly. The housekeeper left the room, closing the door behind her. Josh Carlisle moved to the centre of the room and stood near a high-backed chair, his hand resting on the back.

'Won't you sit down?' Ros said.

This was, after all, his house now, she thought.

'No. I prefer to stand,' he answered. 'Besides, I have something to say to you, Miss Greenway, something I would rather other people didn't hear. I'm only going to say it once, so you had better listen, and listen well.'

Shocked at his tone of voice, Rosalind's eyes widened in amazement. Anger made her ready to attack, and she did.

'Hang on a minute. I'm not one of your servants to be ordered around. I'm not even an employee here, although you may not be aware of that. You can say whatever you've got to say in the presence of anyone in this house. I've got nothing to hide.'

He smiled at her grimly.

'I know exactly what your rôle was in this house, so you needn't come the innocent with me.'

His voice, cold as the moat water, seeped through her defences.

'Play the innocent? Whatever do you mean?'

She stared at him, horrified. He was the person, surely, who should be on the defensive, wasn't he? He was the one who hadn't visited, who hadn't even come to the funeral. What did anyone know about this

9

mystery man, anyway? After Tom's death his solicitor had informed them that Tom's nephew would inherit but couldn't, or wouldn't, tell them any more. She shook her head, trying to clear her jumbled thoughts, desperate to understand what he was saying to her.

'As you are here now, why don't you give me your version of the need for your presence in this house? And for over four months, no less.'

So he knew that much, did he? Rosalind began to relax a little. She was on safe ground. If the man only wanted an explanation of why she was here, there was no problem.

'About five months ago, I was asked by your uncle to come and look at the house, with a view to giving him advice on restoring some of the furnishings and re-decorating a few of the rooms in period. He had the idea of opening the house to the public.'

His eyes narrowed.

'You expect me to believe that? Surely the house is too small to open to the public, isn't it?'

Rosalind warmed to her subject.

'Not at all. The house is a gem. It has hardly changed since it was built, and a Tudor manor house, virtually all of it original, with a moat still in use, would be a great attraction to visitors.'

Her face glowed with enthusiasm and her vivid blue eyes sparkled as she continued.

10

'I could show you what I mean.'

'OK, OK, I get the picture,' he interrupted rudely, 'so let's move on. How come it has taken so long?'

Still puzzled by his attitude, and feeling like she had been caught stealing the family jewels, Rosalind frowned. The work had taken longer than she had originally anticipated and once or twice she had even wondered if Tom was deliberately trying to string it out, finding extra things for her to do. She hadn't made an issue of it, as Tom was her client, but she wasn't about to give this man in front of her a clue about her own doubts.

'Well, naturally, there have been lots of things to organise. The paintings in the portrait gallery, for instance, all had to be cleaned. Tapestries had to be repaired, the drapes on some of the beds were rotting away and had to be replaced. Finding the right materials to use hasn't been easy.'

Nothing had turned out to be easy, but it had been a labour of love for Rosalind. When she first saw the house she had fallen in love with it and had shared Tom's enthusiasm for wanting to restore it.

'And how do you explain having to live here while the work was in progress?' he went on, his voice laden with sarcasm.

'Your uncle asked me to.'

'Bit unusual, wouldn't you say?'

Rosalind felt a blush spreading over her

11

face and had to lower her gaze. Interior designers usually visited their clients frequently to oversee work, unless they were doing it all themselves, and Rosalind was no exception, but Tom had asked her, as a favour, to live in while the work was being done. She had felt awkward at first, but she didn't feel she could refuse. The commission was far too good and, besides, she loved being in the house amongst the beautiful antiques and paintings. It had been no hardship to do as Tom had requested.

She glanced up at this tall, slim man from under her thick dark lashes and shrugged. What could she say? How could she explain that she had sensed loneliness in the older man and a need to be important to someone, and had responded, and they had struck up an almost instant rapport? He had treated her like the daughter he would have loved, but never had. She decided to let this odious creature think what he liked. He was obviously going to, anyway.

'Strange,' he continued, 'when we consider that you already have a home, not twenty miles from here, and could easily have commuted every day. Still living with your parents, I believe.'

Rosalind saw red. So that was his game! Not content with ignoring his uncle himself, he was trying to debase anyone else's friendship with the old man. He even made her sound as if she was sponging off her parents by living with them, and then doing the same to Tom, when the truth was a far cry from what he was suggesting.

'How dare you!' she exclaimed. 'How dare you even think I'm that sort of person.'

'And what sort of person is that, I wonder. Looks suspiciously, to me, like someone taking advantage of a lonely, old man living on his own.'

He came slowly over to where she was standing by the window. With one hand, he reached out to grip her chin, forcing her face around to catch the light. The weak spring sun accentuated the creamy complexion of Rosalind's heart-shaped face and mahogany highlights glinted in the dark mane of hair that framed it.

Unshed tears of anger sparkled in her eyes as she slapped his hand away, wishing wholeheartedly that it was his face. Goaded beyond endurance, Rosalind became very still and, in a quiet voice which friends and relatives would have immediately labelled dangerous, she spoke calmly.

'Of course, you know all about your uncle, don't you? It must have been nice for him, having you visit so often. And so good of you to find the time to come to his funeral, especially with the busy schedule you obviously have!'

Rosalind was gratified to see that his face

had gone pale again. She wanted to hurt him for saying those spiteful, untrue things about her. What did he know about the real situation? Nothing.

'You're just trying to drag my motives, and your uncle's, down to your own pathetic level. He didn't have an unkind bone in his body and would be horrified if he could hear you. I'm not staying here to listen to any more of this,' she said, heading towards the door on shaky legs.

Before she could reach it, there was a knock and Mrs Barnes came in with the tea tray, laid for two. She glanced from one to the other apprehensively before setting it down on a side table.

'Here's your tea, sir,' she said, 'and some of my rich fruit cake. I hope you enjoy it.'

If she noticed the atmosphere in the room, she didn't comment.

'I'm sure I will. Thank you.'

'Well then,' Mrs Barnes said, smiling, 'I'll leave you to it.'

She left, closing the door quietly behind her.

'You can pour,' he said imperiously.

'And you must be deaf or stupid,' Rosalind retorted angrily. 'I've already told you that I'm not staying.'

Privately she thought she would rather be poisoned than stay and drink tea with him. She headed towards the door again, but his next words rooted her to the spot.

14

'I have one last thing to say to you, Miss Greenway. As you seem to be intent on leaving, I shall help you to achieve that aim. I shall expect you to be packed and out of this house by lunchtime tomorrow.'

The words were like a blow to Ros. She had known she would be asked to leave when her commission was completed, but that wasn't to be for another few weeks, and she had already been paid in full. She couldn't afford to give back any of the money she had received, so she would have to stay even if it meant she would be in constant contact with this moron.

She straightened her shoulders, but kept her back to him.

'I have a commission to finish, and I have already been paid.'

'I'm well aware of that. Unfortunately, your presence is required at a meeting here at ten thirty in the morning, otherwise you would be asked to leave now. As soon as it is finished I want you off the premises. Is that understood?'

'Perfectly.'

The bottom had just dropped out of Rosalind's world, but she wouldn't let this man see that. She loved the work she had been doing here, and wanted to specialise in period houses. Completing the commission in order to attract more work of the same kind had been imperative. Now she was not even allowed to finish it, and where would she find the money to pay back?

As she reached the door and opened it, she heard a noise. Turning around, she saw Josh Carlisle, the new owner of Farthings, slide quietly to the floor in a faint.

CHAPTER TWO

It took three of them to get him to bed, putting paid to Ros's theory that if he was slim he must be light. He was all hard muscle she discovered, as they undressed him and got him comfortable.

When she had run for help Ros had been lucky to find Frank, the estate manager, down in the vast kitchen having a cup of tea with Mrs Barnes.

'Thank goodness you are both here,' she said, out of breath from running through the house. 'He's passed out! I need some help, Frank,' she blurted out, gasping for breath as she tried to explain the situation.

The three of them rushed back upstairs to find him still unconscious and very pale, his breathing shallow.

'I think we'll be safe enough to move him before the doctor comes, as he just seems to have passed out,' Ros said. 'We can put him in the Blue Room. It's the nearest, and at least it is finished.'

They lifted the unconscious man and

carried him down the Long Gallery. He groaned as Ros and Frank undressed him as gently as possible while Mrs Barnes bustled off to find a pair of Tom's pyjamas. When she returned, Frank removed Josh's clothes and got him into the pyjamas.

The doctor, who had not only treated Tom but also looked after most of the estate workers, came promptly, and after finishing his examination he joined Ros and Mrs Barnes in the kitchen. After accepting a cup of tea from the housekeeper he leaned back against the Aga.

'He's conscious now, and he's going to be fine,' he said, after sipping from his cup. 'Nothing that a young, healthy body like his can't cope with. He discharged himself from hospital this morning, so really he should be resting up, not driving around the countryside like a lunatic.'

Ros shot him an amazed look. Discharged from hospital, this morning? But why? She couldn't understand why anyone would want to leave hospital before the doctors advised, but he obviously must have had his reasons.

The doctor accepted another cup of tea and a slice of fruit cake.

'Goodness knows why anyone discharges themself before time,' he said, echoing Ros's thoughts. 'He had appendicitis but before they could throw him out, so to speak, there was a complication and he had to go down to the theatre for another operation.'

'Good gracious,' Mrs Barnes said. 'No wonder the poor young man looked so done in when he arrived.'

Poor young man, my eye, Ros thought. If there was anything poor about him, hens must have teeth. He certainly wasn't poor, verbally, but quite able to give as good as he got. She shuddered when she thought about the row they had indulged in earlier. For the time being she would have to keep her views on the new owner of Farthings to herself.

The doctor's words certainly explained a lot, though, like why Josh had hung on to the chair as if it were a lifeline and why he had looked so shaken when the kitten jumped on him. That might also account for his extremely bad temper. Ros perked up at the thought. Perhaps if that was the reason Josh Carlisle was so insufferable, he might not have meant what he said about her having to leave tomorrow. She decided that if he was in a better frame of mind in the morning, she would speak to him again. After all, she had nothing to lose and, with any luck, he might also be having second thoughts about his rudeness to her.

She came out of her reverie to hear the doctor saying, 'Stay in bed for a couple of days at least. The shock to his system of the two operations and his discharge this morning when he really should still be in hospital won't be helping his recovery. I've told him, but what notice a young chap will take of an old saw-bones like me is another matter.'

'Well, we'll just have to make sure he does, won't we, Ros?' Mrs Barnes said, putting on her no-nonsense face.

'We'll certainly try, Mrs B.'

Ros thought this might be more difficult than the housekeeper imagined, but kept her views to herself. She showed the doctor out and, as they made their way to the front door, he asked, 'What do you think the chances are of him staying put?'

'What, in bed? Well, I've only just met him, but I shouldn't think there's much of a chance of Josh Carlisle taking notice of anyone, least of all a woman. If he doesn't want to stay in bed I shouldn't think anyone could persuade him.'

She opened the door and the doctor stood peering out into the early-evening gloom.

'Hm. I rather thought that myself. Oh, well,' he added, 'you'll just have to do your best, Rosalind.'

He began to make his way over the gravel towards the bridge.

'Goodbye, my dear. Give me a ring if you need to.'

Ros's words turned out to be all too true. Frank stayed with the invalid until late evening and Mrs Barnes looked in on him through the night, just to check that he was all right. At four o'clock Ros took over from her so that

Mrs Barnes could get a few hours shut-eye, before everybody wanted their breakfast. Rosalind couldn't sleep. The events of the previous day were still running around in her mind, so she settled herself on a chair near his bed and, angling the bedside light so that it didn't shine on his face, picked up a book to read. The patient was sleeping soundly, and his breathing was regular and even.

Dawn started breaking and, as the sun came up promising another clear, bright day, Ros took stock of the man lying peacefully asleep. Long, dark lashes lay on smooth, tanned cheeks. He looked almost handsome in repose, if you ignored the dark circles under his eyes, which spoke of the considerable pain he must have been in during the last few weeks.

His arms lay on top of the covers and she noticed that the hands had long fingers and square nails. One or two were chipped, as though their owner was used to rough, outdoor work. She was just peering closer, fascinated, when he spoke.

'Need a microscope, Miss Greenway, or can you manage on your own?'

Startled, she sat back on the high-backed chair and looked at his face, a delicate flush suffusing her own.

'You're awake.'

She instantly chided herself. Now she was even making stupid remarks.

'How very perceptive of you.'

20

His brown eyes held hers, bright now with the light of battle. She noticed golden flecks in the brown.

'Next you'll be asking me if I slept well.'

Ros, who had already opened her mouth to do just that, snapped it shut again. Infuriating oaf! I hope he had a terrible night, she thought, mutinously.

The kitten, asleep on the bed, had woken up on the look-out for something to interest him. He obviously thought Josh Carlisle's hand looked a likely snack and promptly pounced on a finger, chewing on the end as if he hadn't eaten for days.

Ros waited for the shout of horror that must surely come. Instead, a rich laugh that seemed to come all the way up from his toes warmed the room and hung in the air. She looked at him, surprised. The smile lit up his face, changing the contours and making him look, if not handsome, certainly extremely attractive. She felt the muscles in her shoulders relax a little in the warmth of the smile, even though it wasn't directed towards her.

'What's the name of this bundle of trouble?' he asked, holding the kitten aloft and depriving it of its imagined breakfast.

'Piglet.'

'Very apt. How come?'

She smiled.

'Tom says . . .'

She stopped when she realised what she had

said. Somehow it was difficult to imagine that Tom wouldn't be saying anything ever again.

'Your uncle said he tries to eat everything that moves, and even some things that don't move, so he thought it was an appropriate name. I suppose he'll stop one day.'

He shook his head.

'Not for some time yet. Burmese cats are known for their inquisitive natures, especially when they are kittens. They jump on door handles and open doors, run up and down curtains, that sort of thing.'

Ros looked horrified, imagining all the precious wall-coverings and curtains that might eventually be thought fair game for sharpening claws on. He laughed at her expression.

'You seem to know an awful lot about the breed,' she commented.

'Not from personal experience, but I wouldn't be worth my weight as a vet if I didn't know much about cats and their habits, would I?'

A vet. It was something Ros hadn't envisaged, yet all the signs were there for her to see—the well-muscled body, hands that were obviously used to hard work, weathered skin from so much time spent out of doors. At least he hadn't been afraid of the kitten yesterday, she thought gratefully, just too ill to do anything about it climbing on his trousers.

'But that won't bother you, will it, Miss

Greenway? After all, you'll be leaving today.'

She was snapped back to the present by his statement. He was rubbing salt into the open wound created by her dismissal. But why? To Rosalind's knowledge they had never met, so how come he was set against her staying? She wished she knew where he had got his knowledge of her. It had been interpreted incorrectly and she would have liked to put the record straight, to make him see that she wasn't the sort of person he obviously thought her to be.

If she was ever going to have his agreement to stay and finish her commission it seemed as good a time as any to ask, while he had it on his mind.

'What you said yesterday about—'

He cut her off by waving a hand imperiously around the room.

'Did you have anything to do with the decoration in this room?'

The smiles and warmth had vanished again, almost as if he regretted showing her even a small part of himself. Ros sighed inwardly. The shutters were certainly down again. She looked around the room at the heavily-carved, oak four-poster bed, the silk drapes which hung from it and matched the ones at the windows, the wallpaper which had been hung for over one hundred years and had just received the attentions of a specialist cleaner, and felt the warm glow of satisfaction in a job well done.

23

'Yes. This was the first room on Tom's schedule that we completed. He even sanctioned the weaving of a carpet especially to tie up the colours and designs. I felt the room could take large areas of blue without feeling cold. It faces south, so catches most of the day's sun.'

A few pieces of porcelain and a couple of vases were shown to advantage on a highly-polished oak table. He gestured towards them.

'Your idea?'

'Yes. There are quite a few lovely pieces around the house. They just needed tying up to the right rooms and furniture.'

'You've done a good job in here.'

'Thank you.'

She glowed in his praise. It could have been a little more fulsome, she felt, but at least it was a start.

'What made you take on this line of work?' he went on.

Always happy to talk about her work, Ros needed no encouragement.

'My parents started me off, I suppose. We've always lived in old houses, not as old as this, but old enough. I read history and art at university. When I came down I took an interior design course and then joined the restoration team of The Embroiderers' Guild, based at Hampton Court. I was there for three years, and loved it. Then I started my own business. And that's it, really.'

He looked at her for some time without speaking. Ros, beginning to feel uncomfortable under his scrutiny, was fishing around in her mind for something to say when Mrs Barnes arrived, bringing in his breakfast tray.

'Good morning, sir,' she said, unfolding the tray legs and then placing it carefully over his knees, 'and a lovely day it is, too. I hope you're feeling better.'

The smells of bacon and freshly-filtered coffee drifted enticingly across to Ros, whose tummy gave an inelegant growl.

'Yes, thank you, Mrs Barnes,' he replied. 'I also have to thank you for keeping an eye on me in the night, I believe. It was a kind thought and I appreciate it.'

Incredible, Ros thought, as she watched the housekeeper pink up prettily under his gaze. It appears he can behave like a human being after all.

'You're welcome, I'm sure.'

Mrs Barnes fussed around smoothing the embroidered tray-cloth and readjusting the cutlery until it was to her satisfaction and then said, 'As the doctor says you won't be able to get up for a day or so, we'll have to find something to keep you amused after breakfast. I'm sure Ros will help.'

He looked past the housekeeper and straight at Ros.

'We'll see about that. Right now why don't

25

you take Ros downstairs and give her some breakfast? It sounds as if she could do with some.'

Downstairs, Ros fed Piglet, who fell on his food as if he hadn't eaten for a week. When it came to her turn she pushed the fluffy, scrambled eggs and toast around on her plate, unable to eat more than a few mouthfuls. Every minute that slipped by was a minute nearer her leaving, and she still hadn't managed to speak to Josh about staying. Would it be possible to change his mind at this late stage, even if she could get him to discuss it with her?

When the ring of the front door bell echoed in the kitchen Ros was on her feet at once, glad of the distraction and anxious to have something to do to keep her mind busy. She was also happy to escape the sympathy of the housekeeper who had been horrified to learn that Ros had been asked to leave.

As she walked along the hall and approached the studded-oak front door whoever was on the other side began to knock on it impatiently. Ros drew back the bolts and pulled the heavy door open.

'About time, too,' the female who stood outside said.

She pushed past Ros in a whirlwind of cloying French perfume.

'And bring in those bags,' she added.

At a loss to figure out who this could be,

and stunned by the woman's attitude, she glanced around the door and noticed two small pieces of luggage sitting on the gravel. The whirlwind divested herself of her black cloak and threw it on to a Victorian porter's chair as if she owned the house and everything in it, including the staff. She revealed a slim body encased in a black polo-neck sweater over tight black trousers. These were tucked into boots which had, Ros noted with horror, three-inch heels.

'Don't just stand there dithering. Shut the door, after you've brought the luggage in, of course.'

Ros was darned if she was going to move a muscle to help this rude woman, whoever she was, and decided to stay put. She supposed that at some time the stranger would say who she was and what she was doing here, but it would be without Ros's help. The object of her thoughts checked her reflection in the gilt-edged mirror hanging on the wall and patted her smooth, blonde hair.

'Well, get on with it.'

Ros left the luggage where it was, shut the door and turned to the woman.

'Are you expected?' Ros asked.

'Where is he, anyway?'

'Where is who?'

Ros's fingers itched with the thought of grabbing the overbearing woman by the shoulders and shaking her until her teeth

27

rattled. Shocked at the thought, she clasped her hands behind her back, as if by this very act the feeling would go away.

'Josh, of course,' the woman said, looking as though she were amazed that Ros even needed to ask the question.

Obviously, Ros thought irreverently. Who else in the house could possibly be associated with someone like this? With such appalling manners in common they had to be related.

'Mr Carlisle is still in bed, I believe. If you would care to tell me who you are I'll see that he is told of your arrival.'

'There'll be no need for that. I'm Mrs Carlisle and I'll tell him myself.'

She turned towards the staircase.

His wife! Ros fought down dismay at the revelation. It couldn't be true, surely. He couldn't be married to this odious, overbearing creature, could he? She got a grip on herself. What does it matter to me to whom he is married? It's not as if I am interested in him anyway, she thought, shrugging off the remembrance of his warm smile earlier in the morning. She wished them joy of each other!

Nevertheless, Rosalind had the urge to take the woman down a peg or two. In a couple of hours I shall be gone, she thought, and someone should at least make a small dent in this woman's ego. She smiled to herself. What did she have to lose?

'Mrs Carlisle, I'm afraid I will have to ask

28

you to take off your shoes and put on a pair of house slippers,' Ros said, pointing to a rack standing on one side of the hall, full of cotton mules in different sizes, each pair wrapped hygienically. 'I'm sure you won't be aware, but this is a very old house and small heels can seriously damage the oak flooring. Mr Bradshaw always asked visitors to put them on.'

The thought of this woman having to exchange three inches for a pair of flat mules, and serviceable cotton ones at that, was very satisfying. In fact, the prospect was getting more interesting by the second as she studied the woman's figure and saw that without the advantage of the boots her legs would appear to be too short for her body. As Ros's own legs, according to her family, went way up past her waist, she anticipated a delicious sense of one-upmanship.'

She pretended to make a show of looking at the other woman's feet and then said, 'I'm not sure if we have a pair big enough, though.'

Had she been there, Mrs Barnes could have cut the atmosphere with one of her well-sharpened kitchen knives. At the bottom of the stairs the blonde turned and threw an icy glance at Ros.

'But surely you are forgetting two important things, aren't you?'

Her voice was saccharine sweet.

'Mr Bradshaw is dead and I'm not a visitor.

So I think I'll just ignore your request.'

'I wouldn't if I were you.'

The two women turned, as one, towards the voice. Josh Carlisle was leaning against the rail and its supporting carved balusters halfway down the wide staircase. Ros wondered how long he had been there, listening. The blonde was first to recover.

'Josh, darling,' she purred, running up the stairs separating them and planting a kiss on his face as she wrapped her arms around him.

'I've missed you,' she said in a whimpering voice.

Ros saw him wince. He shouldn't be out of bed, she realised. He'll have another relapse if he isn't careful.

'Hello, June. You're early. I didn't expect you till lunch time. Did you bring Robert with you?'

The smile left her face.

'No. He had to go out early, so I came on my own. This person refused to bring in my bags.'

She pointed down the stairs to where Ros stood in the hall.

'There aren't any servants here, June. If you want them brought in you'll have to do it yourself or leave them for Robert later.'

'But it looks like it's going to rain,' she said, pouting at him.

Josh, who must have already seen the clear, bright sky that morning gave her a withering look.

'Then it'll just have to get wet, won't it?'

Ros watched, fascinated. If this was marriage, it was certainly like none she had seen before. Her parents bickered from time to time, but it was always the friendly kind, and they made up afterwards. She had the feeling that there wouldn't be much making up between these two.

Josh untangled the blonde and made his way slowly down the stairs.

'Put the slippers on, June, and I'll ask Mrs Barnes to find you a room. Ros can show you where it is.'

June flounced down the stairs, deliberately ignoring Ros as she passed. While Ros waited for her to find a pair of mules to fit, she heard Josh talking to Mrs Barnes about room allocations. It did seem a bit strange to Ros that he didn't want her to share the room he was in, but it made sense. The bed in the Blue Room, although high and intricately carved, only gave the impression of being a big bed. It was, in fact, quite a small double. If he was still in considerable discomfort, as appeared to be the case, he would find it difficult sharing that bed.

Josh and Mrs Barnes came along the passage from the kitchen and she introduced herself.

'If you would like to come with me, Mrs Carlisle, I'll show you to your room.'

The two women started upstairs, June having retrieved her cases from outside with obvious reluctance.

'Oh, and by the way, Mrs Barnes,' Josh said, 'there will be ten of us, including yourself, at the meeting. Could you arrange chairs in whatever room you think suitable, please? And coffee afterwards, I think.'

'Yes, sir, of course,' Mrs Barnes said.

He turned to Ros.

'Now, if you will excuse me.'

He started to walk away.

'But I thought we might—' Ros began.

'I'm sorry,' he said, 'I've got Frank waiting to see me. I can't stop.'

He turned on his heel and walked away in the direction of the office. Ros had the feeling he was trying to avoid her. He was making it very clear that he didn't want any discussion with her at all. She saw the chance of completing her commission vanish totally and, with a heavy heart, she made her way up to the room which she had come to look on as hers.

Last night she had taken everything to do with the work on the house along to her work-room and laid it out methodically so that whoever took over could see, at a glance, what was still to be done. Lists were made of the items which were out of the house being restored, what firms held certain pieces of furniture and the names of the companies who still had to come to the house for on-the-spot restoration work.

She fingered the swatches of materials and her coloured line-drawings of how the rooms would look when they were completed, and was sad. How she would love to have been able to see the final results. Now she finished packing, not even aware of carefully folding each garment and laying them in her suitcases. She was numb with disappointment. Unable to face anyone else at present she sat on her bed and looked out of the window until it was time for the meeting.

Rosalind was at a loss to understand why she had to go to the meeting. Considering Carlisle was virtually throwing her out of the house, she couldn't see the reason for her attendance.

Mrs Barnes had obviously decided that the library was the room most suitable for the meeting, and had laid out the chairs facing a large desk which stood in front of the big mullion windows. The room was looking at its best. A fire was alight in the hearth and a large copper bowl planted up with brightly-coloured primulas sat in the middle of a reading table. Sunlight streamed in through the windows.

Ros had always liked this room. It was one of the few rooms in the house to have been modernised, although whether anyone would call an alteration done in the Georgian period modernised was debatable. Every available wall was covered with bookcases built by a master craftsman. Made in yew, over the years their colour had mellowed to tawny and when the sun shone in, as it did now, the wood seemed to glow.

The cases were full of Tom's collection of first editions standing cheek by jowl with what he used to call his penny dreadfuls, the paperbacks he loved to read and re-read until they were falling to bits.

Already in the room when Ros went in were Frank, the estate manager, and his wife, together with Mrs Barnes, two of the estate workers who had been with Tom for years, the farm manager, Ben, and his wife, Sarah. Ros was greeted warmly by everyone. Mrs Barnes had obviously been talking as most of them already knew that Ros had been asked to leave and they all wanted to say how sorry they were to hear of her imminent departure. Commiseration was cut short by the arrival of their new boss together with Tom's solicitor.

'Perhaps you would all like to sit down, ladies and gentlemen,' Josh said.

The staff moved to sit down, Mrs Barnes drawing Ros over to sit next to her. Under cover of the general disturbance Ros whispered to her.

'What are we here for? Any idea?'

'The will, of course. The solicitor is here to read the will.'

'But this has got nothing to do with me. I shouldn't be here.'

She stood up to leave, desperate to be away before the meeting started, but Mrs Barnes pulled her back to her seat, patted her in a motherly fashion and was just about to say something when Josh spoke.

'I have asked you all here this morning so that the solicitor can read my uncle's will. Naturally, I already know the contents.'

Naturally, Ros thought sarcastically. She looked round the room and was surprised to discover that Mrs Carlisle wasn't there.

'As my uncle asked that you should all be together when told,' Josh was saying, 'I have done this as soon as possible. As some of you may know, I was in hospital until yesterday, which left me unable to attend his funeral, as I would have wished.'

He looked directly at Ros as he said this. She flushed and looked away.

OK, so I got it wrong, she conceded. Why on earth didn't he tell me that yesterday, though, when I flung those accusations at him? She fumed silently, her fingers itching to wipe the know-it-all look off his face. If it was his intention to make her look small, he was going about it in the right way. And what was worse, she realised, she would have to apologise to him later.

That still didn't excuse the man for not visiting his uncle when he was still alive, she maintained bitterly. It's easy to go to a funeral when you know you have been left an estate and millions as well, but what about caring for your relatives when they were alive? Coming from a close-knit family herself, Ros couldn't understand people who were sometimes out of touch with their relatives for years at a time. And now, surprise, surprise, here he was on the scene at just the right time to claim his inheritance. How convenient.

The solicitor was on his feet now, rustling through some papers he had taken from his briefcase. Ros listened as he outlined the bequests for Tom's most loyal staff, and remembered how bountiful Tom had been in life, as he was now being in death. The money and gifts left to his staff, many of whom had become good friends to him, were extremely generous. Ros was genuinely pleased for them.

Her pleasure was short-lived, however, when she heard her own name, and what she heard shocked her to her very roots.

'And to Miss Rosalind Greenway I leave the sum of five hundred thousand pounds, to do with as she . . .'

CHAPTER THREE

A strangled cry left Rosalind's throat. She knew that if she hadn't already been sitting down she would have fallen. Her mouth went dry and she found breathing almost impossible. The shock of the solicitor's words drove every thought from her mind as she tried to take in the enormity of the situation. That he should have left her anything at all was a surprise, but such a large amount was almost incomprehensible.

Suddenly everything began to fall into place. This must be why Josh was so rude to her yesterday. He must have hated his uncle leaving her such a large sum, especially when he knew that they hadn't known each other for long. Her eyes were drawn to where he stood near the window. He was looking straight at her, dark eyebrows curling down in a frown over piercing eyes. Ros shut her own eyes in an effort to blot out the sight.

She wished she knew why he was looking at her like that. He had just finished telling everybody that he knew the contents of the will, so why the frown? He knew that Tom had left her this large amount of money, so what was bothering him, other than the fact that he probably resented it?

The solicitor droned on for a few minutes more, everything he said going straight over the top of Ros's head. She was numb. There had been so many shocks in the past twenty-four hours, and this the worst of them all. She would have to give it back. How could she possibly keep the money knowing how hostile Josh was about her legacy? And what had Tom been thinking about, leaving her so much?

Mrs Barnes, noticing her agitation, leaned towards her sympathetically.

'Are you all right, dear?' she whispered. 'You've gone very pale.'

Ros ran a shaky hand through her hair and turned to the housekeeper.

'Why did Tom do it? Why has he left me anything, let alone such a large sum? There has to be a mistake.'

Mrs Barnes smiled at her.

'No, dear. Mr Tom wouldn't make a mistake like that. He was very fond of you, you know. Thought the world of you, he did. We all saw that. Used to tell me he would have loved a daughter like you.'

She patted her arm.

'He was a very generous man.'

Ros had to get out of the room and be on her own for a while. She couldn't bear the thought of having to speak to anyone else just yet. Eventually the solicitor would have to be contacted and the legacy refused, but just now her priority was to get out of the house as fast as possible. Josh Carlisle said a few words and brought the meeting to an end.

The staff began to relax, to move about and talk to each other, delighted with their good fortune. Mrs Barnes left the room to make the coffee and Josh appeared to be deep in conversation with the solicitor. Ros saw this as a perfect opportunity to slip out of the room unseen and leave the house. She desperately needed to be on her own, to come to terms with all that had happened. With Josh busy with the solicitor and not looking in her direction she saw her chance of slipping away unseen, and headed for the door. She was opening it when a hand grabbed her arm in a grip like steel.

'I want to speak to you,' Josh demanded, forcing her to turn around.

She glanced up at him, eyes pleading.

'I don't know what to say.'

He shot her a long, hard look and seemed to come to a decision.

'I've still got to talk to some of the others. Come and have coffee and we can talk later.'

Ros looked away from him and nodded. He moved back from her, letting his hand drop from her arm. She waited until he had his back to her and was walking away, then slipped out of the door and went to her room to collect her cases, still in a daze. Thank goodness they are packed and waiting, she thought, as she picked up her coat from the bed and put it on.

Having a last look around the room to make sure she had remembered everything, Ros caught sight of herself in the ornate gilt mirror. Her eyes appeared huge in her face, her complexion now drained of colour. She looked away hurriedly, picked up her cases and made her way downstairs. Choosing the back staircase to avoid going down the Long Gallery and past the library, she gave a sigh of relief as she reached the front door without seeing anyone and let herself out into the late-morning sunshine.

She felt sad at not being able to say goodbye to Mrs Barnes and the others, but she could phone later and give her apologies. Nothing was going to keep her in this house a moment longer than necessary. Her feet scrunched on the gravel as she walked towards the bridge over the moat, refusing to allow herself one last look at the beautiful, old house. It would have been too painful. She wanted to remember it as a happy house, which it had been when Tom was alive.

Although the sun still shone in a cloudless sky a chilly breeze had sprung up and Ros shivered as she crossed the bridge and made her way to the garages. She had opened the doors and was unlocking the boot of her car when she heard a noise and spun around. Josh Carlisle was outlined against the light from outside the garages and was breathing heavily as though he had been running, which he must have been, she realised, to have got here so fast.

'Where do you think you are going?' he asked, walking into the garage and coming to stand in front of her.

She noticed that his colour was high. He must have been pushing himself to the limit. She didn't reply to his question.

'Well?' he repeated.

'You told me to leave. So I'm leaving.'

She lifted a suitcase and almost threw it into the boot of her car.

'I told you after the meeting that I wanted to talk to you,' he said, exasperation in his voice. 'And stop that!'

He grabbed the second suitcase that had been on its way to join the first and put it down on the ground again.

'Look,' Ros said, anger overriding the bad shock she had just had. 'You may want to speak to me but, quite frankly, I don't want to speak to you. Since you arrived in this house yesterday your attitude towards me has been one of rudeness and arrogance. You treated me as if I was something the cat had brought in, and obviously had already made up your mind as to what sort of person you thought I was.'

Violet eyes flashed angrily.

'And now your uncle, through his will, has put me in an intolerable situation. You've probably had a good laugh at my expense, but I'm leaving now and, hopefully, in time, I shall be able to forget that the last two days ever existed.'

She reached out for the case sitting on the ground.

'You're not going anywhere.'

Josh grabbed her arm and pulled her away from the car. His hands moved up to her arms and gripped her shoulders. Ros was dismayed

41

to discover that she was shaking uncontrollably.

'Look, for what it's worth, I didn't know about the money. It came as a complete shock to me this morning to learn that Tom had left me anything at all, let alone such a large amount. Of course I don't expect you to believe me, but it's the truth. Besides, I'm not going to accept it.'

'What do you mean, not accept it?'

He must have realised he was hurting her as his grip relaxed.

'How would Tom feel if he knew you were rejecting his gift? Anyway, you can't do that.'

'I can't do what?'

'Give it back. You can't give back a legacy.'

'Can't I?'

'No,' he replied smugly.

'Oh.'

His reply threw her for a moment, unsure as she was on legal matters. What if he was right and she had to keep it? She decided to say nothing more until she had checked it out with a solicitor.

'And what about the commission?' he was saying now.

Ros looked up, dazed, to brown eyes flecked with gold. Their expression was softer than she had seen them previously and she wondered what was going on in his mind.

'What about it?'

'You still haven't finished the work.'

Her shoulders drooped and she closed her eyes briefly and sighed. The man was impossible.

'I can't keep up with you. You know darn well it isn't finished because you told me not to!'

A flicker of a smile passed over his face.

'I've changed my mind. So you had better get back and finish it, hadn't you?'

She stared at him, now totally bemused.

'What in heaven's name do you want? One minute you tell me to leave without finishing the work, now you tell me I have to stay.'

Was she ever going to understand him?

'And what if I refuse?'

He pulled her slowly towards him and when his face was just inches from hers he said, quietly, 'Then, Miss Greenway, I shall just have to sue you for breach of contract, won't I?'

For a second Ros couldn't think of a thing to say. She couldn't take her eyes off his face. He seemed to be looking right into her soul. His voice was telling her one thing, yet his body seemed to be saying something completely different. Ros was afraid she was misreading the signals he was sending out. He moved closer. He surely couldn't be going to kiss her, could he? Her legs felt weak and her mouth suddenly went dry.

Outside, the birds might have been singing and the wind sighing in the trees, but inside the garage the only sound Ros could hear was her heart beating. Needing to steady herself, her hands burrowed inside his jacket and clung to his waist for support. It felt good, touching his shirt warmed by his well-muscled body. She knew he was going to kiss her and, against her will, she found herself wanting to respond to him. His eyes glowed with tawny lights as his mouth started the downward journey to hers. His lips were cool and soft on hers. They were interrupted by a laconic, masculine voice.

'Well, well. I do so hope I am interrupting something interesting.'

Ros opened her eyes and looked at Josh. He froze for an instant, his eyes becoming hard and uncompromising. He released her and turned towards the voice, keeping his body between Ros and the newcomer, for which she was grateful.

She leaned against the car in an effort to gather her scattered thoughts. Realisation of what she had been doing hit her. He was married, for goodness' sake. He shouldn't have been kissing her but, she had to admit, she shouldn't have let him, either. Whatever was she thinking about? That was just it, though, she chided herself. She hadn't been thinking. One show of interest from this man she kept telling herself she didn't even like, and she was lost.

She shook her head in disbelief. What sort of woman was she turning into? And now this stranger had seen what had happened between them and put two and two together. By the sound of it he had managed to come up with an answer of four.

'So, you finally arrived,' Josh said. 'June's been here all morning. What took you so long?'

'Now that's a nice brotherly greeting, if ever I heard one,' the man said. 'Don't I even get an introduction?'

Ros took a deep breath and moved around Josh to look at the stranger, who stared right back and gave a low whistle.

'Wow! Looks like you hit the jackpot this time, dear boy. Has June met this one yet? I can't imagine she will be very happy.'

He held out his hand and smiled.

'As my brother is sadly lacking in manners, I can see that I shall have to do the necessary myself.'

Josh moved closer to Ros.

'As you will probably have gathered, Ros, this is my brother. Robert, this is Miss Rosalind Greenway, who has been working on the house.'

'Twin, actually,' Robert said. 'Not identical, as you will have noticed,' he said, correctly interpreting Ros's surprised look.

A person less like a twin it would be hard to find, she thought, noticing the shorter height, the fair, sandy hair and the downwards droop to the mouth. He looked as if he expected life

45

to have thrown riches at him and considered it a personal affront that he had been passed by. The only vague similarity was in their eyes, both brown. But whereas Josh had tawny flecks, his sibling's appeared to be flat and cold.

Ros shook hands with the brother.

'How do you do, Mr Carlisle?'

'Robert, please. I'm sure we're going to be the best of friends. But do the cases mean that you are leaving us already?'

He gestured towards the suitcase in the boot.

'No, it doesn't,' Josh returned. 'Rosalind and I were just discussing the continuation of her work here, when you arrived.'

'And a fascinating discussion it seemed, too.'

Ros glanced at Josh. A muscle throbbed in his neck and she could feel the anger emanating from him. He took a step towards his brother.

'Back off, Robert.'

'OK,' Robert said. 'No offence, besides, I need help. The car's broken down at the gates. I've had to walk up, and a long, thirsty walk it was, too.'

Josh took some keys from his pocket and threw them at his brother, who caught them.

'Take my car. It's in the next garage. You can bring back your things and then call a service garage from the house.'

Robert turned towards the next garage

without a word. Neither of them moved until they heard the car reverse out of the garage and disappear away down the drive. Then Josh turned to her.

'Well? Are you staying or going?'

What a wonderful choice, Ros thought. He's threatening to sue me if I don't stay and finish the work, and if I do stay it'll be like living in a hornets' nest, waiting to see who stings me first, his wife, his brother, or him.

And what if he made another pass at her? At close quarters she found him disturbingly attractive. Ros didn't know whether she would have the strength, or the inclination to stop him, and this worried her. But she knew it wasn't a choice at all. If her career was to continue along the lines she wanted she would have to finish this commission. There was no room for unprofessionalism in her life. She sighed.

'I'm staying, but only until the commission is completed.'

Did she imagine it, or was there a lessening of tension in the garage?

'Of course. That goes without saying. Let's get these things back to the house then.'

He picked up the cases and headed out of the garage. Ros locked her car and ran after him.

'Here, let me help. You shouldn't be carrying those yet. Not so soon after your op, anyway.'

47

He sent her a scathing look.

'I don't need your sympathy.'

'It wasn't sympathy,' Ros replied. 'Just an offer of help.'

They retraced their steps in silence over the bridge and across the gravel towards the house. Inside, he put down the cases. She noticed his colour was still high. Carrying the cases had surely been too much, too soon, but Ros decided to keep her mouth shut. If he wanted to push himself beyond his limit, that was his affair.

'I shall expect you to join us for lunch in half an hour.'

'Oh, but I was going to have it with—'

'Where did you have your meals when my uncle was alive?' he interrupted.

'With Tom,' she said reluctantly.

She remembered their shared meals with affection. Tom Bradshaw had an alert, intelligent mind and they often had heated discussions ranging over a wide variety of subjects. They never worried about which side of the fence they were on. Sometimes Ros would play devil's advocate, sometimes Tom would, purely for the enjoyment of a friendly argument.

'Then there's no problem?' he asked and Ros shook her head.

'Good. In normal circumstances we will just grab a sandwich at lunchtime and eat in the evening. I shall expect you to eat with me. As

48

this is the start of a new venture and my family is here, I feel we should make an exception today. Half an hour, then.'

He nodded in her direction and turned towards the passage that led to the office.

'Oh, by the way, I almost forgot, this is for you.'

He fished in his pocket and pulled out a folded envelope.

'It's from Tom.'

She turned the envelope over in her hands as he walked away, and noticed her name written in Tom's bold handwriting. Ros stared down at it. It jolted her, and she felt his presence as she clutched the letter in her hand. She wished there could be some way of having him alive again, whatever the cost, and that the last two days had never happened.

Alone, surrounded by her luggage, she felt like a piece of flotsam that had been caught in the sluice gates at the end of the moat, and abandoned there when the river level dropped.

She reached the drawing-room later with two minutes to spare. June Carlisle was sitting in a comfortable chintz-covered armchair next to the crackling fire, showing a great deal of leg. She had obviously spent a large chunk of her morning re-doing an already perfect make-up. Not a hair was out of place. She had also changed, and was wearing a tight-skirted black dress whose neckline plunged dramatically.

Ros's eyes sparkled when she noticed that

49

June was still wearing the cotton mules from this morning. Flat shoes were obviously not an item in her wardrobe. It somehow made nonsense of her attempt at sophistication. At the same time, Ros was very aware that her half-hour had been spent unpacking, and she had just had time to drag a comb through her unruly mane before coming down. Her own outfit of a soft violet cashmere sweater and corduroy skirt to match might have been a birthday gift from her parents a few years ago, but set off her eyes to perfection, a fact not wasted on Robert, if his rapt attention was anything to go on.

The two men were standing at the drink trolley. Josh, in the process of pouring a drink for his brother, turned to her.

'Good. You're here. May I offer you a drink?'

She shook her head, then changed her mind.

'Well, just a fruit juice, then.'

'Oh, surely not,' Robert said. 'This is a celebration, after all. Go on, have something a bit more daring.'

'Don't force her, darling,' June said, in a condescending voice. 'She probably can't hold it.'

Ros made herself keep walking towards the men and came to a stop in front of Josh. He was looking at her like a big cat waiting for its prey to make a false move so that it could pounce. Only the tawny lights in his eyes betrayed his inner laughter. He raised one eyebrow and waited. She felt her mouth twitch upwards at the corners and turned to beam a smile in Robert's direction.

'If you are all celebrating, who am I to put a damper on things? I'll have a white port, as long as it is chilled,' she said.

She saw Josh turn towards the drinks and sort through the bottles, a half-smile on his face. Ros felt a mad surge of excitement sweep over her. He liked her reply. On a scale of one to ten that must surely rate as three Brownie points, she estimated, hugging the thought to her.

Mrs Barnes arrived shortly afterwards to tell them lunch was ready, and they moved through to the dining-room. The table had been laid with heavy silver cutlery and antique lace place mats, and the sparkle of the hand-cut crystal wine glasses reflected in the table's polished surface.

They started with chilled almond soup decorated with flaked almonds and whipped lemon cream accompanied by small, warm, plaited-bread rolls topped with poppy seeds.

'Mrs Barnes is a gem,' Ros said, finishing her soup. 'I shall never be able to face baked beans again after food like this.'

'But you will be glad to leave here, I am sure. I expect you have to watch your weight quite carefully, don't you?' June said. 'It's such a bore, isn't it? Fortunately I never have to watch mine, unlike some people.'

She smiled smugly at Ros and twirled her wine glass around by the stem.

Ros, who had never even inclined towards plumpness, knew exactly what June was up to, but refused to be drawn and stayed silent.

June continued, 'I understand you will be leaving quite soon.'

'It will be at least two months before Rosalind leaves. There is still quite a large part of her commission to finish,' Josh answered. 'You will have to get used to her being around.'

Ros looked his way in some surprise. This was news to her. There was, perhaps, three weeks to a month's work at the most, providing the outside contractors finished their restorations on time, and she certainly hadn't had time even to discuss the time-scale with him. So far he hadn't shown the slightest interest in anything to do with her or the work, except trying to get her to leave. Did he know something that she didn't, or was he just baiting his wife? She pondered this for a while as their salmon poached in white wine and tarragon arrived, and Josh poured the Australian Chardonnay to accompany it.

'Robert, I think it would be a good idea if you went over the estate this afternoon with Frank,' he said, as Ros spooned baby new potatoes on to her plate and handed the bowl to Robert. 'He says he will stay until Michaelmas, which gives us six months, but you need to get accustomed to the system as soon as possible.'

'Frank is leaving?' Ros asked, shocked by the news. 'But why? He has been here for years.'

'Just so,' Josh said. 'He feels he's too old to be able to work under a new owner and wants to take early retirement. Robert is taking over.'

Robert, who had been drinking continuously since before lunch, turned to her and, in a belligerent voice said, 'Is there any reason why I shouldn't?'

'Of course not,' Ros said, horrified by her outburst. 'I'm sorry. I didn't mean to appear rude. It's certainly nothing to do with me, but it was just a shock to hear that he was leaving.'

June looked at her.

'You are right, for once. It isn't anything to do with you. Besides, by rights, Robert should own half this estate. After all, he and Josh are twins. Why the old fool had to leave it all to Josh I really don't know.'

Josh frowned at her and laid down his knife and fork.

'June, I've already told you, this is not a subject for discussion and certainly not outside the family.'

'She's right, all the same,' Robert threw in, refilling his glass. 'Why should I have to be someone else's lackey, while you sit back and enjoy the millions he left? He must have known you were one of twins, so why should you have it all?'

Josh rubbed a hand tiredly over his face. He was going to have his work cut out managing these two, Ros thought. They were like vipers, using their tongues where they could do most damage.

They finished the meal in silence, everyone refusing the pudding. As Ros stirred cream into her coffee she mulled over what she had heard and felt decidedly uncomfortable. Robert and June seemed intent on dragging personalities into every topic of conversation. Hopefully she wouldn't be seeing much of them in her day-to-day work. She couldn't understand the other woman at all. Why would she want to give Robert half the estate? June gave the impression that she would be quite ruthless when it came to money, and not worry whose toes she stepped on to get it. Something here didn't seem quite right. Perhaps she had a secret wish that Josh was Robert. It was certainly apparent that her marriage was not good and perhaps now she was just staying for the money. Unscrupulous women did that, Ros knew.

Ignoring their previous comments, Josh said, 'Frank will show you the cottage that will be available at the end of next week. You can use that until he leaves and then you can move into the farmhouse.'

June leaned over and covered Josh's hand with her own.

'But, Josh, darling, I thought we would be living in the house here, not miles from anywhere in some silly, little cottage.'

Josh pulled his hand away from hers.

'That's not possible, June. Besides, you knew the score before you agreed to come. As Robert will be running the estate and overseeing the farm, he needs to be on hand.'

Robert got unsteadily to his feet.

'Come, dear wife, it sounds like we have been given our orders, so we must obey.'

Ros, in the process of downing a mouthful of coffee, choked. She couldn't believe what she had heard. Wife? June was actually Robert's wife and not Josh's? Her coughing fit was ignored by June and Robert, who left the room. She took a handkerchief from her pocket and mopped the tears at the corners of her eyes. Josh, elbows on table, hands nursing his coffee cup, waited for her to recover.

'OK now?'

Ros nodded. She tried to speak but her throat was too sore and all she could manage was a croak. He seemed to know exactly what was going on in her mind, and appeared to be amused by it. How could she have been so dim? But then, remembering back to when June arrived she had certainly been given the impression that June was married to Josh, and

June had been happy to let people keep that impression. A spot of wishful thinking, perhaps? Josh hadn't exactly told anyone otherwise, either.

'This afternoon,' Josh said, 'I have to drive over to my practice to see my partner and my locum who has been standing in for me since I've been in hospital, so I won't be around. I'll catch up with you later and we can discuss your work then.'

Ros cleared her throat, about to offer to drive him herself, but thought better of it.

'Yes, of course.'

He rose to his feet and started towards the door.

'Disappointed?' he asked, as he came to a stop opposite her.

'Me? Why should I be?'

He smiled, though there was no warmth in it.

'I thought you might be sorry that I wasn't married to June. First wealthy widowers and now married men, hm?'

His meaning hit Ros like a sledgehammer. He actually thought that Tom had left her the money for services rendered and that she had instigated the kiss between them in the garage earlier in the morning, as though she were nothing more than a tart! A hot flush swept over her face. She jumped to her feet, knocking over her chair in the process.

'Who do you think you are?' she stormed

at him, clutching the edge of the table for support. 'You arrogant, overbearing, insufferable . . .'

Words failed her. Angry tears threatened to spill over her lashes and run down her cheeks.

'You know absolutely nothing about the situation between Tom and me, and now you are trying to blame me for what happened this morning! How dare you! What about your own conduct?'

She had to admit to herself that some of the anger she felt was caused by guilt. She had believed him to be married when he kissed her, yet didn't want to stop him, so what did that make her? His laugh was cruel.

'A first-class performance, if I may say so. I'd have to give you ten out of ten for effort.'

Ros had to get out of the room before she said anything more or perhaps even did something silly, like throw something at him. Hands clenched and held rigidly at her sides she walked around the table and past him with as much dignity as she could dredge up. She continued out of the door and up to her workroom, head up and back ramrod straight. The last thing she would do was let him see how badly his words had shocked her.

It was some time later that Ros looked around and realised where she was. It didn't surprise her. Work had always been a comfort to her and often in the past she found her worries and problems helped by switching off and concentrating on the work in hand. This afternoon was no exception. It was as though a tornado had ripped through her body leaving nothing but a shell, an empty, numb shell. She idly picked up a piece of embroidery waiting for repair and gently moved the pads of her fingers over the silk threads. They had a reassuring feel to them, and it wasn't long before Ros was hunting through her silks to find a matching tone for the repair.

Lifting her head some time later and glancing at her watch Ros was amazed to find that the whole afternoon had passed. She flexed her fingers and did a few neck and shoulder exercises to ease her muscles. The light was fading as Mrs Barnes arrived with a pot of tea. She was thrilled that Josh had seen sense, as she put it, and decided to let Rosalind finish her commission. But Ros couldn't respond properly, feeling as she did that it was a mixed blessing.

When the housekeeper had gone and Ros sipped the hot brew, she remembered Tom's letter, still squashed in her pocket. She took it out and turned it over several times, almost afraid to open it as feelings that she had held back for the past few weeks threatened to swamp her. Carefully slitting the envelope, she reverently pulled out the single sheet of paper covered in Tom's bold handwriting and began to read.

My dear Rosalind, it began, *since you are*

*reading this you will already know that I am
dead. I hope that we will have had many years of
happy friendship before this time, but only God
can see that far ahead. You have brought warmth
to this house that has not been here since my late
wife died. Edith would have loved you for your
sunny nature and marvellous sense of humour,
the daughter we never had.*

*I do hope, my dear, knowing your fiercely
independent streak, that you won't be too cross
with me for leaving what is, to me, a relatively
small gift. I truly hope that you will enjoy
spending the money as much as I enjoyed giving
it to you.*

Yours, Tom.

Ros saw that the letter was dated just four
days before his stroke. It proved to be the final
straw and the emotions of the last two days
closed in and swallowed her. A large tear
rolled down her face and splashed on to the
letter in her shaking hands.

Some time later, strong hands gripped her
shoulders and turned her around, pulling her
against rough tweed. Through her misery Ros
recognised it as the jacket Josh had worn that
morning. He had pulled up a chair and was
sitting next to her. She breathed in the faint
smell of citrus aftershave as he pulled her
against him, strong arms wrapping themselves
around her as protection. The tears flowed on.

'What happened, Ros? Can you talk about
it?'

She shook her head almost imperceptibly. He seemed to understand. Gradually the tears subsided and she felt him gently kiss the top of her hair before easing her away from him and drying her tears with a handkerchief. Ros was embarrassed to be near him after the thoughts he had obviously been harbouring about her but lacking energy and feeling increasingly fragile, his sympathy was her undoing.

She looked at him, eyes full of pain. He kissed her forehead and then, softly, her cheek. Her eyes closed, tension easing out of her body, hands slowly releasing their stranglehold on his jacket. She felt safe and comfortable in his arms. It was impossible to pull back as he lowered his mouth to hers. She needed the comfort he was offering, was going to take whatever he gave for the moment. The future would have to go hang.

CHAPTER FOUR

His kisses were growing in intensity when suddenly he pushed Ros away from him, stood up and walked across the room to the window. She watched his progress with growing confusion, her skin still tingling with the excitement of his kisses.

She sensed his annoyance, but couldn't understand it. Surely something that felt so right couldn't be bad? Was he blaming her for what happened between them? He had been bitingly rude to her at lunchtime, practically accusing her of getting his uncle's money under false pretences and chasing any man she met. And now she had helped him fix that picture more firmly in his mind by responding to his kisses without thought or hesitation. She shook her head, unable to understand her own rash behaviour.

Dusk had fallen and the light in the room bounced Josh's reflection back at her from the small, diamond-shaped panes. Keeping his back to her and his eyes fixed on the window, he ran a hand distractedly through his hair.

'Rosalind, I'm sorry. That was unforgivable of me.'

His words surprised her. She had thought he would blame her yet again. An apology was the last thing she expected to hear. Briefly looking over his shoulder at her before returning his gaze to the window, he continued.

'You were upset and I took advantage of that.'

His words had the ring of truth, but Ros was honest enough to admit that she hadn't exactly pushed him away.

'Josh, I really don't think you can be entirely to blame.'

'No,' he interrupted, 'don't try to make excuses for me. Whatever I think of your motives for doing what you have in the past, I had no right to force myself on you.'

Rosalind smiled wryly. Force, indeed. She felt the warmth of a blush steal over her face and thought of her own willingness to be taken advantage of. He turned away from the window, pushing his hands in his jacket pockets and walked over to the table.

Nodding in the direction of the letter he asked, 'Is that what upset you?'

'Yes.'

She quickly picked up the letter, folded it and held it to her. The contents were too painful for her to let anyone read it, least of all the man who was determined to see nothing good in her relationship with his uncle.

'Is it from my uncle?' he asked.

She nodded.

'I see,' he said.

Ros looked up at him in time to see dark brows furrow together in a thunderous frown, his expression closed and forbidding. She sighed. Josh had obviously come to his own conclusions and, as usual, they were wrong.

'No, you don't see at all,' she retaliated, angry with him now for continually misunderstanding her. 'You are determined to deliberately misinterpret the relationship between Tom and me.'

'Oh, really?' Josh interrupted.

'There's no reason for sarcasm, either. As I was about to say, I cared for your uncle a great deal, which is more than can be said for you!'

Ros bit her lip, suddenly afraid she might have said too much, and cross with Josh for having caught her off balance. As she watched, his expression changed. He didn't look guilty at all, as she had expected, just very sad.

'Who says I didn't care for my uncle?'

'Well,' Ros said, floundering a little, 'it's perfectly obvious, isn't it?'

'Why? Because I didn't come to his funeral?'

'No, not that,' Ros said, waving a hand dismissively at him. 'You already said you were in hospital and, besides, it's what we do for people when they are alive that counts, not what we do when they are dead.'

'So what makes you think I didn't care for him?' Josh asked quietly.

Ros wondered how she had managed to get into this corner, but knew that she had burned her boats, metaphorically. She might as well say it all.

'Tom was a darling. A kinder, more generous man you couldn't wish to meet. Everyone who knew him loved him, and yet you couldn't even be bothered to visit.'

She was well into her stride now, unable to stop even if she had wanted to. The weeks of anger and disappointment she had felt on Tom's behalf all came flooding to the surface.

'Yet he still left virtually everything to you, though you couldn't even force yourself to come to see him. What sort of person are

63

you?'

Josh's face paled and his eyes glittered angrily, making his quiet words all the more forceful.

'I don't suppose you want to deal in the truth, Miss Know-It-All, seeing how you prefer to make up what you know about me but, for your information, until last month, I didn't even know I had an uncle!'

He waited for the words to sink in.

'Now, what do you make of that?' he asked eventually.

Ros looked at him in startled amazement.

'Not know? That's—'

But Josh wasn't listening to her any more. He strode to the door, threw it back on its hinges and walked out, leaving Ros staring into space, her mouth open. She shut it with a snap and sat down abruptly. Minutes passed before her brain stopped whirling uselessly and she could begin to go over what he had said. He didn't know he had an uncle? How could that be? Surely Tom Bradshaw would never have left his money to someone who didn't even know of his existence. Tom obviously knew about Josh, so how come Josh didn't know about Tom?

She had no time to make sense of one question before another popped into her mind. It was all too much for Rosalind. If what Josh had said was true, and she had no reason to think he was lying, then she had just made the most awful fool of herself. She looked down and was surprised to see Tom's letter screwed into a tight ball in her hand, the result of her anger.

'Oh, Tom, what have I done?' she whispered as she smoothed out the single sheet, folded it neatly and replaced it in its envelope. 'How am I going to be able to face him now?'

Still feeling numb, Ros tidied up her work and made her way downstairs to the kitchen with her tea tray. She knew it would be impossible to sit at the same table as Josh that evening and was racking her brains for an excuse to avoid having to see him when, luckily, she had help from an unexpected quarter. In the kitchen she found Mrs Barnes banging pots around on top of the Aga, her back and shoulders rigid with anger. June, looking equally angry, was standing in the middle of the kitchen floor, facing her. Enticing smells of lamb and rosemary were wafting around the kitchen.

'When will you be able to do it then?' June asked.

'I've already told you,' Mrs Barnes said, busy stirring the contents of a saucepan. 'Even if I had all the ingredients, which I don't, it's too late to be cooking that for dinner.'

'You've said that already,' June argued, totally ignoring Ros, 'so I shall expect it tomorrow then.'

65

Mrs Barnes turned on June, her face pink with agitation.

'Perhaps not.'

She caught sight of Ros rinsing her teapot in the sink and gave a gasp.

'My dear girl, whatever is wrong? You look terrible.'

'Thanks, Mrs Barnes.'

Mrs Barnes steered Ros across the kitchen to a chair.

'Sit down there for a minute, chick, and tell me how you feel.'

Ros didn't have time to answer before Mrs Barnes peered at her closely and spoke again.

'I think you are coming down with something. Don't you think she is coming down with something?'

She turned to June, their row seemingly forgotten in the new turn of events. Exasperated that the conversation wasn't in her control any longer, June came forward a few steps and looked at Ros.

'She looks awful, I agree.'

Rosalind wasn't surprised at the other woman's answer. She had a feeling that June would have told any woman they looked awful if she had an opportunity.

'Bed for you,' Mrs Barnes said, looking at Ros. 'It could be flu.'

'I totally agree,' June said. 'We don't want to catch whatever it is you've got. Anyway, the family has important things to discuss tonight, so it's probably just as well that you won't be around. Now, I must go. I've got better things to do than stand here gossiping.'

She left the room and Mrs Barnes raised her eyes skyward.

'That woman is going to get the sharp end of my tongue one of these days.'

'It sounded as if you were putting her in her place when I came in,' Ros said, shivering.

The housekeeper noticed. Going over to a cupboard she started to move bottles about on the shelves, talking as she busied herself.

'Coming in here and trying to tell me what to cook! I ask you! As if what I've been doing for the last seventeen years for Mr Tom isn't good enough for her. Besides, she will only be in the house for another few weeks, so she'll have to put up with what she gets.'

She took a bottle of brandy from the cupboard, fetched a glass and poured a measure.

'Here you are. Get this inside you. It'll help to ward off anything that might be imminent,' she said, handing her the glass.

'Honestly, Mrs B,' Ros said, feeling guilty at being made such a fuss of, 'I don't need this. I'm sure I'm not coming down with anything.'

'You didn't see yourself when you walked in here. If you want my opinion it's all them shocks you've been having these last two days.'

She sat down at the table opposite.

'First he wants you to go, then he wants you

to stay. Then Mr Tom leaves you all that money you weren't expecting. It's enough to knock anyone sideways.'

Ros was surprised at the housekeeper's shrewd assessment of the situation. If only that was all there was to it, she thought, staring gloomily through the amber liquid to the bottom of the glass.

'It won't do you any good staring at it, young lady.'

'I hate brandy.'

'You're not supposed to like medicine. Now, quick, down the hatch.'

Ros did as she was told and swallowed the brandy in a couple of gulps, screwing up her face as the fiery liquid hit the back of her throat.

'Yuck.'

'Right, bed for you now. Have a warm bath and tuck yourself in and in a while I'll bring you up something to eat.'

'I'll definitely take your advice and have an early night, but I don't think I could eat a thing, and I certainly don't want you to be waiting on me when you're so busy,' Ros said.

'Dinner is all under control, so you don't need to worry about that,' Mrs Barnes said shooing Ros out the door. 'You just go and have a nice bath. Put plenty of bubbles in, that'll cheer you up.'

They hadn't exactly cheered Ros up, she reflected later, propped up in bed, but at least she felt calm and more in control of her feelings.

Mrs Barnes surprised her with a supper tray. Some seafood pasta and a green salad sat cheek-by-jowl with a glass of chilled wine and a helping of light lemon mousse with lemon sauce. When the housekeeper left her with the tray she didn't know if she would be able to eat very much but knew she would have to try a few mouthfuls to appease Mrs Barnes. She forked some pasta, which was delicious, and thought about the events of the day, trying to put them into perspective. She ate as she relived everything that had happened and soon every scrap of food had disappeared.

There was nothing for it. She was going to have to apologise to Josh yet again. Why couldn't she ever keep quiet she wondered, instead of jumping in with her own views before she knew all the facts. In future she would have to keep her mouth shut, and her feelings to herself. She sighed. That might prove to be difficult, knowing her fiery temper, but she would have to make a serious effort.

It was none of her business, after all. If Josh hadn't known he had an uncle there wasn't a lot she could do about it. It was sad that he had missed knowing such a lovely man as Tom, but that was all in the past.

Having got that straight in her mind, Ros felt a whole lot better. She put the empty tray on top of her dressing table, snuggled down in the bed, closed her eyes and was asleep in minutes.

CHAPTER FIVE

She knocked gently on the door and opened it. The family records room was small. Inside, the walls were lined with shelves stacked from top to bottom with files, boxes and bundles of papers, some with ribbon or held together with string. This room held most of the legal and household papers concerning the house and estate, some hundreds of years old.

Josh was sitting in the old leather chair which was cracked and scarred with age and shiny with use. Ros had seen Tom sitting in it so often before. She swallowed hard, trying to put the memory out of her mind. Josh was the new owner of Farthings now. Ros knew that things had to move forward. Even so, it was hard to see the younger man in the place of the old.

At a small desk in front of the window a large bowl of blue hyacinths sweetly scented the tiny room, their flowers caught in a patch of weak early-morning sunshine.

'Can you spare a minute?' Ros asked.

Josh had been poring over some papers, which were lying on the desk. He turned at the sound of her voice.

'Yes, of course. Come on in and have a seat,' he said.

He looked solemn and Ros's heart felt as though it had plummeted down to her shoes. He must still be cross with me for my outburst last night, she thought. He moved some papers off the only other chair in the room so that Ros could sit down, and they both started to speak at the same time.

'Look, I'm really—'

'Josh, I've got—'

They smiled tentatively at each other.

'Age should always give way to beauty, so you first,' Josh said.

Ros took a deep breath, wanting her apology over as quickly as possible.

'Josh, I've got to apologise for those terrible things I said to you yesterday. They were totally—'

'No,' Josh interrupted. 'You've got nothing to apologise for.'

'But I have,' Ros said. 'I said some awful things and I had no right. I had no idea that you didn't know your uncle.'

He smiled wryly at her.

'After I left you and had time to calm down a bit, I thought over what you said and, more importantly, the way you said it and how you looked. I've seen a cat protecting her kittens look at me like that.'

'Have you?' Ros said in surprise.

'Yes. I came to the conclusion that you

71

weren't angry with me on your own account, but for Tom's. Am I right?'

She nodded and looked away, unable to speak.

'You really cared about him, didn't you?'

'I've never denied that, Josh.'

'No, you haven't. I even tried to make something sordid out of your friendship with him. I'm sorry for that and I hope you will forgive me.'

Ros felt as though a huge weight had been lifted from her. Seeing the seriousness of his expression and his attempt to make amends, she smiled.

'Of course I do.'

'Good. It's just that I was . . . well . . .'

He shrugged his shoulders.

'It doesn't matter now.'

Ros wondered what he had been going to say. He leaned across the small gap between them and took her hands in his.

'Rosalind, if you feel up to it, would you tell me what he was like? What sort of person was he? Tell me everything you know about him.'

'That's a tall order,' she said. 'There's not much I can tell you that you won't hear from his staff and I was only here for four months, as you know.'

He squeezed her hands.

'Just give me your honest opinions. That's all I'm asking for.'

She smiled again.

'You're on, but, Josh, I have to ask, how come you didn't know he existed?'

Ros thought of her own close-knit family and couldn't envisage not knowing all her aunts and uncles, cousins, nephews and nieces.

He sat back in the leather chair.

'My father was in the Army. He died in active service when Robert and I were quite young and my mother had a hard struggle bringing us up. She always told us she had no relatives.'

'But why?'

He lifted his shoulders expressively.

'Perhaps she and Tom fell out. Who knows why people do what they do? Anyway, it wasn't until her death last month that I knew she had a brother.'

This was news to Ros. She was appalled to think that he had only just lost his mother, too, and now his uncle. It must have been a terrible blow for him to learn he had a relative he didn't know about, only to have him taken away again. She wanted to sympathise, but didn't want to interrupt.

'Going through her bureau after her death I found some old letters to her from Tom. They must have been sent after my father was killed, because Tom offered to pay for my schooling and to see me through university. I don't know what my mother wrote to him, but in the next letter he said he was sorry that she had refused help, as, naturally, he would want to do it for me as I was the eldest and one day would inherit everything he had. There wasn't an offer to do it for Robert, too, though.'

'You'd have thought that your mother would have been delighted,' Ros said. 'It must have been difficult for her, financially, with two young sons to educate.'

'There were a couple of letters after that from Tom saying something along the lines that he was sorry she had taken that attitude and was refusing to answer his letters. Then nothing.'

He looked at his watch and jumped to his feet.

'Look, let's get some fresh air. I've got a great deal to discover about the estate and I want to walk across to the home farm this morning. You can talk while we walk, unless you have more important things to do, that is.'

She smiled up at him, happy to meet him halfway in his efforts to get on with her.

'I'd like that. I'll just go and get a coat.'

The weak sun shone fitfully through fast-moving clouds propelled across the sky by a chilly wind as they left the house. Rosalind tied her bright red scarf closer round her throat and pulled her matching woollen hat lower over her ears. They walked along the rain-sodden lane towards the farm. Although it hadn't been raining for the last few days the ground hadn't started to recover from a winter of almost continuous rain.

Josh strode out and Rosalind had to increase her stride to keep up with him. He stopped suddenly and, gripping her arm, pointed towards the field they were just passing. Ros turned in the direction of his gaze. Looking over the five-bar gate she could make out a herd of Highland cattle meandering slowly across the field, pulling up tufts of early-spring grass as they went.

'Doesn't that strike you as odd?' he asked.

She raised her eyebrows questioningly.

'What?'

'Highland cattle in the middle of Sussex, of course,' he said, moving over to the gate and leaning on it. 'They are far more suited to the hills of Scotland than the lowlands of Sussex. So why here? Any ideas?'

Ros joined him at the gate and looked at the animals in the field.

'Yes. It was Tom's idea. His wife, Edith, your aunt, was a Scot. Years of living in England didn't stop her from being homesick from time to time, although Tom said she tried to hide it. Anyway, he bought a herd of them for her birthday one year and didn't tell her. On the morning of her birthday Tom just told her to look out of the window, and there they were.'

Ros smiled as she remembered Tom telling her how thrilled and surprised Edith had been.

'Tom got interested in them after a while and started to breed them. He told me he won quite a few prizes at shows. He even took to riding one.'

'Riding?'

The look of genuine surprise on Josh's face made Rosalind laugh.

'Yes, so he said. Not recently, of course, but some years ago. Apparently one of them was quite biddable and Tom called him Hamish. He used to saddle up Hamish and ride all over the farm on him. Comfier than a horse, Tom said, but more difficult to control.'

Josh started to laugh and Ros joined in.

'He also said that sometimes they ended up somewhere completely different from where he was trying to go. One day Hamish trampled a whole bed of Edith's favourite roses in the formal garden before Tom could manoeuvre him away.'

The nearest cattle, hearing their voices, had wandered over to inspect the two people. They crowded around the gate, jostling each other, creating miniature patches of fog where their warm breath hit the cold morning air. Big, curved horns and long, shaggy hair that covered their eyes made them appear ferocious, but their noses when they leaned towards Ros to touch her outstretched hands, were gentle. She turned to Josh and smiled.

'Beautiful, aren't they?'

He was gazing raptly at her.

'Yes, very beautiful.'

His eyes didn't leave her face and she had

the strangest feeling he wasn't talking about the cattle. Embarrassed, she glanced away. Just then they heard the sound of a Land-Rover coming along the lane. The driver had obviously noticed them, as the vehicle slowed, then stopped at the gate.

June climbed down from the driver's seat and Ros felt a distinct chill settle in the air. She wondered, as she glanced at the tight skirt, high-heeled boots and expensive jacket the other woman was wearing, if June would ever settle down to being an estate manager's wife. She couldn't see it.

June glanced from one to the other before picking her way carefully over the wet ground to where Josh stood at the gate.

'Darling, I've been looking for you everywhere,' she said, managing, in one fluid movement, to stand between them, turn her back on Ros and link her arm with Josh's.

'I need some help. There seems to be no water at this terrible little cottage you've decided Rob and I have to live in, so you'll have to come and do something about it.'

'Where's Frank?' Josh asked. 'He'll fix it for you.'

'How should I know? Probably chewing on a piece of straw somewhere.'

Josh's voice was cold as he answered her.

'I doubt that he will be doing that. Frank works very hard, June, as you will soon discover when Rob takes over his work.'

'Sorry. Anyway, will you please come and sort out this water thing?'

She looked over her shoulder at Ros and threw a saccharine smile in her direction.

'You will probably be wanting to get back to work, won't you?'

'Well, I . . .'

June turned back to Josh.

'There, that's settled then. Come on.'

She started to pull on his arm, but Josh disengaged himself.

'Go and wait in the Land-Rover, June. I'll be there in a minute.'

June smirked and tottered off towards the vehicle. Josh turned to Ros and raised his eyebrows.

'I'm sorry about this, Ros, but I'll have to go and sort this out.'

'It's OK, really,' she said. 'I understand.'

He gave her a wintry smile.

'That's more than I do then.'

Moving over to her, he took her hand in his, gave it a quick squeeze and walked away.

What had started out as a promising day had been spoiled by June's appearance. Ros sighed. She knew she would have to try to get on with Josh's sister-in-law, if only to make life easier for herself until her commission was finished, but she knew it would be an uphill struggle. The woman was determined not to like her. Ros turned away from the gate and made her way back to the house and her work.

The following week passed slowly for Ros. She avoided Josh and June by eating all her meals in the kitchen with Mrs Barnes. Josh was extremely busy trying to understand the business his uncle had left him, and used to collapse into bed, shattered, at all hours of the night, according to Mrs Barnes. He didn't seek Ros out to ask why she wasn't eating with the family any more, and for that she was grateful.

She did wonder, from time to time, whether he realised what June was up to. If Josh couldn't see the truth for himself that was his problem. She certainly wasn't going to get dragged into their family squabbles any more.

The rain continued to fall relentlessly from a leaden sky, depressing her normally buoyant spirits. Her daily walks in the garden had to be curtailed because the ground was so waterlogged and her work was proving to be less of an absorbing interest than it had been. In short, Rosalind was distracted.

She took the opportunity to spend the weekend at home with her parents and sisters, Beatrice and Katherine, their high spirits and energy helping to throw off her own lethargy, so that by the time she got back to Farthings late on Sunday night, she was feeling happier than she had done for days.

Next morning, down in the kitchen, Mrs Barnes was busy taking a pan of sausages and bacon out of the Aga. Frank, the estate manager, who had been at work since six o'clock, had come over to the house as usual for breakfast and was sitting at the table finishing off a plateful of cereal.

' 'Morning everybody,' Ros said, sniffing appreciatively at the freshly-filtered coffee aroma that permeated the room.

Frank mumbled, ' 'Mornin',' through a mouthful of cereal and Mrs Barnes beamed in her direction.

'Well, I must say, you look a whole lot better this morning, chick,' she said, resting one hand on her hip and surveying Ros.

'I feel it, too. A weekend at home always cheers me up.'

'More than can be said for that lot,' Mrs Barnes said, jerking a thumb in the direction of the closed kitchen door.

'Oh?' Ros said, shaking some cereal into a bowl. 'What have I missed?'

Mrs Barnes dished up the sausages and bacon, added an egg and some baked tomatoes to the plate and put it in front of Frank.

'Come on then, Agnes,' Frank said to Mrs Barnes. 'Don't keep the girl in suspense.'

Mrs Barnes continued.

'They've been at each other's throats all weekend. If it wasn't Mrs High-and-Mighty shouting at her husband it was him shouting at Mr Josh, poor soul, and Mr Josh shouting right back.'

Rosalind tried to squash the smile that

80

threatened to sneak from the corners of her mouth. Poor soul, indeed.

'June's in a right tizzy because she and Robert have to move out of the house today, now the cottage is ready for them.'

Frank was chuckling away to himself.

'That's a bit sudden, isn't it?' Ros asked.

'No,' Frank said. 'Mr Josh has had people running around all over the cottage during the week, painters, carpenters and carpet-fitters. He told them they had to be finished by today otherwise they wouldn't get paid, so one of the painters told me.'

Ros was surprised at the speed with which Josh had obviously moved to get June and Robert into their new home. No wonder she hadn't seen much of him during the week. He must have been up at the cottage, organising the workers.

'And, what's more,' Mrs Barnes said as she cut large slices of bread and fitted them into the toasting iron, 'Mr Josh came in here in a great flap on Saturday morning. Said he had just seen your car going down the drive, and where were you going? I told him you were going home for the weekend, but nothing would do but for him to check your workroom to make sure the work was in progress. Then he had me take a peek in your room to make sure your clothes were there.'

She eyed Ros knowingly.

'Must have thought you had left

81

permanently.'

Ros blushed guiltily. The thought had crossed her mind frequently during the past week.

'I don't think I would have done that without telling him, Mrs B.'

'That's what I said. Anyway, he'll have his hands full for the next few weeks with Frank on holiday.'

Ros looked at Frank.

'When are you off?'

'This afternoon. The wife and I are travelling down to her sister's. She lives near the airport, so we can stay the night with her and be ready for our early-morning flight.'

He shook his head.

'I'm worried about the brother, though.'

'Oh? Why?' Ros asked, accepting a cup of coffee from Mrs Barnes.

'He's supposed to be taking over from me in September. That gives him plenty of time to start learning the ropes, but his heart isn't in it. We've got a very good farm manager, as you know, so it isn't even as if he has to deal with the day-to-day running of the farm, but he just doesn't seem to be interested in the other areas of the job.'

Frank munched on some toast and swallowed a mouthful of tea before continuing.

'Things like making sure the tenants of our properties in the village are paying their rents, keeping the estate workers busy, maintaining the buildings, that sort of thing. And on Saturday morning he wasn't too steady on his feet, if you know what I mean.'

'Is it any wonder?' Mrs Barnes said, disgustedly, as she poured tea for herself and sat down at the table. 'With the amount he drinks at dinner each night I'm surprised he can stand up at all.'

Ros agreed wholeheartedly with them, but knew it wouldn't do to voice her opinions. She was worried, nevertheless.

'Frank, why don't you stay on then, instead of leaving? I'm sure Mr Carlisle would be delighted if you told him you have changed your mind.'

Frank sighed.

'I know it must have seemed a bit of a sudden decision, but I couldn't work for someone different after being with Mr Tom for so long. Thirty-five years it's been, you know. Also, when Mr Tom passed on we didn't know anything about the new owner, did we? Although I must admit that Mr Josh is a good man and, in time, will probably be as good for the estate as Mr Tom was.'

He scratched his head.

'The missus is very sad to be leaving our house and the friends we have made over the years, but I couldn't stay, especially not if the brother was around, putting his foot in everything. Besides, I'm almost at retiring age.'

Frank finished his cup of tea, got to his feet and patted Mrs Barnes' shoulder as he passed her chair.

'Thanks for breakfast, Agnes.'

He took his jacket and cap off the hook on the kitchen door, shrugged himself into his jacket and said, 'See you both when I get back, then.'

'Have a lovely time, Frank,' Ros said, 'and try not to worry about the place while you are away.'

Josh's arrival in her workroom later that afternoon was a surprise to Ros. He came in quietly and startled her.

'Hello.'

She smiled, her heart doing somersaults at the sight of him. He came over to her worktable and perched on the edge, one leg swinging.

'Did you have a good weekend? Mrs Barnes told me you went home.'

'Yes, lovely thanks.'

Ros went on sewing, trying not to feel excited. Although they had run into each other and said the odd word in passing, this was the first time he had sought her out in almost a week, and she didn't want to say anything to make him go away angry.

'Good. I expect you have heard that June and Robert are moving into their cottage today.'

'Yes, I did. June will miss this lovely old

house, I expect,' Ros said.

'I don't really think June is capable of appreciating all this,' Josh said, 'but at least it will get her out from under my feet.'

Ros quickly looked down at the work on her lap hoping that he hadn't seen her surprised expression. The last time he had discussed June with her it had been to defend her. What had happened since then to make him change his mind?

'I know what you are thinking,' he said, 'that she must have had some encouragement from me to behave the way she did. But I never took her behaviour towards me seriously. It became apparent to me that June and Robert would have to move out sooner, rather than later, so that I could distance myself from her. Though, goodness knows where she got the idea that I could ever be anything other than a brother-in-law to her.'

Ros thought privately that, at some time, June must have regretted marrying the wrong brother, probably still did.

'But that's all in the past,' Josh said. 'Right now I want to know why you have been avoiding me.'

'I thought it might be prudent to keep out of the way for a while,' Ros said, laying her needlework down and abandoning all pretence of working.

Josh grinned.

'What you really mean is, you were fed up

of being accused of things you hadn't done and fed up with the family bickering.'

Ros couldn't help smiling.

'Something like that.'

'If I promise not to do it again, will you say I am forgiven?'

I could forgive you anything, Ros thought, as he took her hand and laced his fingers through hers.

'What do you say?'

'A promise?' she said.

'I take my promises very seriously, Ros,' he said quietly.

'Then I accept.'

Bringing her hand to his lips he kissed the palm lightly.

'Thank goodness,' he breathed.

The nerve endings on Ros's palm tingled as his lips met her skin and electric currents seemed to run up her arm and through her body. He bent his head towards her and Ros went weak with anticipation. Just as his lips met hers the door to the workroom was unceremoniously thrown open and June walked in. Josh was the first to recover.

'What happened to the old-fashioned idea of knocking on the door first, June?'

Ros tried to pull her hand away from Josh, but he held her firm.

'I thought I was entering someone's workroom. I didn't expect to see some sordid little—' June began.

'That's quite enough!'

Josh's fingers dug into Ros's hand.

'Your opinion of what is going on here is of no interest to us. Say what you came to say and then go.'

June was patently startled by his outburst and Ros realised that he did indeed have his sister-in-law's measure at last. When June spoke again it was with a subdued voice.

'You said to tell you when all our luggage was packed. You did promise to help me get it over to the cottage.'

'Yes, so I did. I'll come straight away.'

He turned to Ros and smiled.

'Tonight I have been asked out for a meal, but we'll have dinner together tomorrow evening, if that's OK with you.'

Ros could only nod in agreement.

He smiled at her, bent to place a gentle kiss on her lips and was gone.

Rosalind passed the next half-hour gazing into space and re-living every minute that Josh had spent with her and every word he said. Her feelings for him were becoming deeper and she began to hope that he might feel the same way about her. It was obvious that he was attracted to her, at least that was a start, but how deep did his affections run?

Realising that there was no chance of concentrating on her needlework for the rest of the day, Ros had started to tidy it away when she heard a noise. Turning, she saw June standing in the doorway. Startled by the woman's reappearance Ros jumped to her feet.

'I thought you had gone to the cottage with Josh.'

June ventured into the room.

'Yes, I was supposed to be but, clever me, I managed to load the Land-Rover so there was no room for me. Josh has had to take the luggage and come back for me again.'

Her smile was pure vitriol. She came across to where Ros was standing.

'Besides, we have unfinished business, I think.'

'Not that I am aware,' Ros said, gripping the edge of the table.

'Yes, we have, and it's all your fault,' June started. 'If it hadn't been for you, Josh would be eating out of my hand by now. I should be living in this house, not you.'

Ros tried to interrupt.

'But I'm only here—'

'You're all over him,' June went on. 'Don't think I haven't noticed. I don't plan for all that money to go to some little nobody like you. That money is as much mine as it is Josh's. Robert is his twin and should get at least half of it. I mean to see he does, so keep away from our family.'

'I'm not after his money, as you so crudely put it,' Ros retaliated.

June's breathing had become ragged, her

88

eyes glassy and Ros wondered if there was any chance of getting out of the room without a fight. June was clearly beside herself with rage.

'Don't think he is going to take any notice of you,' June said. 'A few kisses don't mean anything.'

'What happens between Josh and me is none of your business, as he has already told you,' Ros retorted. 'If you've nothing further to say perhaps you would leave now.'

She raised her chin and pulled back her shoulders, hoping the body language would get through to June and show that she wasn't afraid of her. Inside, she was shaking and her knuckles were white where they gripped the table.

'I'm going, but I'll tell you this much about him,' June said bitterly, her breath catching a sob. 'He's not capable of loving anyone! I should know.'

CHAPTER SIX

Getting no response, June turned around and flounced towards the door, with the parting shot as she left, 'Don't say I didn't warn you.'

Ros took a few deep breaths to try to calm herself. She righted the chair that had fallen over and slowly sat down on it again. Had June been telling the truth? Yet how could he have been so loving towards her if he was incapable of loving anyone?

Getting to her feet she paced up and down the room. Perhaps a few kisses, to some men, didn't mean anything very much. A sharp stab of pain ran through her at the very idea that Josh was like other men. He couldn't be. After all, hadn't he told her himself that he took his promises seriously? He seemed to be an honourable person, but what did she really know of him? They had been in each other's company for such a short time yet she had felt, instinctively, that he had been genuine in his dealings with her, even when sounding off for something he thought she had done.

She smiled wryly, or hadn't she always followed her instincts? Perhaps I should take a bit more notice of logic, she told herself as she moved over to the window and stared out. Dusk was falling now, darkness creeping over the moat towards the house.

The following afternoon, Rosalind took advantage of a change in the weather to get some exercise. Although the rain had stopped, a cool wind was blowing and she walked briskly along the lane which ran between Farthings and the estate farm in an attempt to keep warm. Glad to be out in the fresh air again after so many days indoors, she looked around her with interest. Spring was slow to put in its appearance this year and the fields were sodden, the trees showing few buds.

As she neared the farmyard, a Land-Rover came careering down the lane towards her and braked sharply. The driver wound down the window and stuck his head out. It was Ben, the young farm manager.

'Ros,' he called, beckoning her over. 'Thank goodness I've found somebody sensible.'

Ros laughed.

'Hello, Ben. I'm not sure about the sensible bit, though,' she joked as she crossed the lane to the vehicle.

'You'll have to do.'

Ben looked at her anxiously.

Sensing something was wrong, Ros said, 'What's the problem?'

Ben gestured his head in the direction of the passenger seat, where his heavily-pregnant wife, Sarah, was sitting.

'It's Sarah. She's gone into labour. I'm on my way to the hospital now.'

Ros looked across at the young woman.

'Are you all right, Sarah? Do you need some help?'

The young woman shook her head.

'The baby isn't due for another three weeks. I'm sure I'll be OK, just as long as Ben gets a move on.'

'That's where you come in, Ros,' Ben said. 'I've tried to call Mr Carlisle on his mobile, but the number is constantly engaged. The lads are scattered over various parts of the farm today and, what do you know, Bessy has decided to go into labour at the same time.'

He threw up his hands in mock despair.

'Why you women can't get better organised, I don't know.'

Ros couldn't help laughing. Harloco Beswick, better known as Bessy, was a Highland heifer and had been Tom's pride and joy. Three years old now, this was to be her first offspring. When Tom was alive he had taken Ros to meet her and she had fallen instantly in love with the young animal. He had bred Bessy himself, and had taken delight in pointing out her finer points to Ros, showing with pride the rosettes she had won when competing at shows with her mother. Tom would have been looking forward, with excitement, to the birth.

'I found Robert and asked him to take her over to the small barn,' Ben said. 'If she's on her own she shouldn't get too over-excited, but she really needs someone to keep an eye on her, especially as this is her first. Normally I, or one of the boys, would do it but as I've got to get to the hospital with Sarah, Mr Carlisle will have to keep an eye on her.'

A sharp cry came from the other side of the Land-Rover as Sarah doubled up in pain.

'For goodness' sake, don't hang around, Ben. I'll find Josh and tell him about Bessy. You just get Sarah to the hospital,' Ros exclaimed anxiously.

'Thanks.'

He didn't need any second bidding.

'Good luck,' Ros shouted as Ben headed the Land-Rover up the lane in the direction of the nearest town and its hospital.

Ros decided to go back to the house and find Josh. She had started to walk back down the lane when she thought about going to take a look at Bessy, not that she knew anything about animals giving birth, but it would be lovely to see the new baby when it arrived. Better not, she decided. Her first task must be to find Josh and tell him what had happened.

Back at the house, all was quiet. Josh was nowhere to be found and even Mrs Barnes was out. Rosalind looked everywhere she could think of, without luck. Pulling off her gloves and stuffing them into the pockets of her jacket she found some paper and scribbled notes explaining the situation. She left them in the kitchen, Frank's office, where Josh spent a lot of his time, and the records room. At least he would find one of them sooner or later.

At last she tried phoning his mobile but it was still engaged, as Ben had found earlier. She looked at her watch. Three o'clock. Another four hours before Josh would expect her for dinner, if she decided to go. Outdoors again, she pulled on her gloves against the cold afternoon and decided to walk back to the farm and have a look at Bessy. Her spirits lifted as she thought about the cow that had been Tom's favourite, and wondered if it was

93

going to be a heifer or a bullock. She knew Tom had been hoping for a heifer to continue his breeding programme.

Ros strode purposefully up the lane again towards the barn. Inside, Bessy was tied up to a wall and turned at Ros's approach. She walked towards the heifer and talked to her quietly as she moved.

'Hello, Bessy, old girl. How are you feeling?'

She came to a stop at her side and ran a hand slowly down the animal's back.

'Not long to go now.'

The animal moved restlessly on its floor of straw.

'Well, well, if it isn't the lady decorator, come to give us the benefit of her experience of calving, no doubt.'

Ros turned in the direction of the voice and could just make out a head, tucked down amongst a stack of straw bales at the far end of the barn. It was Robert. The rest of his body was out of sight behind the bales. She went over to him.

'Hello, Robert.'

She looked down and saw that he had made a bed of sorts for himself and was lying on it.

'I've just come to see Bessy,' she added.

'Know her personally, do you?'

Ros ignored his sarcasm.

'Yes, I do, actually.'

'I thought you had come to see me.'

Robert scrabbled around at his side and

94

picked up a full-size bottle of vodka, which had been hidden in the straw. Ros noticed it was almost empty. He waved the bottle at her, offering her a drink.

She shook her head. Robert was supposed to be looking out for the cow, making sure she wasn't in any sort of trouble and yet, here he was, virtually drunk and it not even three-thirty in the afternoon. He patted the straw, indicating that Ros would sit down beside him. She perched instead on an upturned straw bale.

'Now, isn't this cosy? Just you and me and a bottle,' Robert slurred.

Ros wondered just how much of the bottle he had managed to consume that day. Quite a lot if the level of alcohol remaining was anything to go by.

He crawled over to where Ros was sitting and grasped her ankle.

'Why don't you come down here, gorgeous, and we can get better acquainted? You know, I've always wanted to get to know you better, Ros, as well as my brother does, if not better. How about it, hm?'

She jumped to her feet, backing off a few paces out of his reach.

'I came to see how Bessy is, Robert, nothing more.'

She tried to keep calm.

'How is she, anyway?'

'How the heck should I know? I don't know

the first thing about nursemaiding cows, and I'm not about to start learning, either.'

Ros looked down at him in disgust, and wondered how two brothers, twins even, could grow up to be so different. Just then she heard a noise behind her and turned to see that Bessy had gone down in the straw and was lying on her side. She rushed over to the animal which seemed to be distressed. She noticed that the chain by which the animal was tethered was too short, and Bessy's head was off the ground, pulled upright by the chain.

Ros looked at the chain and saw that it was attached to the wall by a bolt and she knew it would be impossible to release it without the right equipment. She kneeled down by the animal's head and ran her hands along the chain around its neck, talking calmly to it while doing so. There was no chance of getting the chain off from that end, either, as it was deeply embedded in Bessy's hair and almost strangling her. What a pity she hadn't been tied up with that length of rope lying on the floor, Ros thought.

'Why is she tied up on this chain?' she asked Robert. 'I thought they were usually tied up with rope.'

Robert pulled himself to his feet and leaned against the wall. The vodka bottle fell out of his hand. At least he can't drink any more, Ros thought thankfully, as she saw it fall.

'Better on a chain than a rope. They run off,

don't they?'

Ros began to feel panicky. She tried to squash the feeling as it rose in her, knowing she had to keep calm for the animal's sake. Even if Robert was sober they could never move her on their own.

'Robert, I think she's in real trouble. We must get someone here as soon as possible, preferably a vet. Have you any idea where Josh is?'

' 'Course not. The god of the veterinary world doesn't favour his lowly subjects with such mundane details as to where he is, or what he does.'

Ros closed her eyes and sighed. Talking to Robert was useless. She had never seen him so drunk, and was amazed at the depth of the animosity he seemed to have for his brother. It was almost as if he hated Josh. This is getting me nowhere, she thought. Concentrate. You've got a sick animal here needing attention. Forget Robert. Do something!

Rising to her feet and brushing straw off her trousers, she turned towards Robert and was horrified to see that he had just lit a cigarette. She saw him inhale deeply and put his lighter back in his pocket. The crass stupidity of the man. Was he too drunk to know what he was doing?

'Are you totally brainless?' she ground out. 'Have you any idea what danger you are putting us all in, you fool?' she said, shaking with fury.

His mouth dropped open in surprise, the cigarette almost falling out.

'Now, just a minute, I'm not putting anyone at risk.'

'Oh, no?' Ros interrupted. 'Look around you and tell me what you see.'

He lifted his shoulders in a shrug and dragged on his cigarette.

'Then let me tell you what I see,' Ros said, pointing around the inside of the barn. 'I see an animal in distress unable to help itself, I see straw everywhere, I see an old building and I see a drunk, smoking a cigarette.'

'There's no need to be churlish, just because I made a pass at you. Some women would have been delighted. And I'm certainly not drunk.'

'I don't think anyone would believe you, Robert.'

Ros was holding on to her temper by a thread.

'I'm going to look for help for Bessy. Make sure that by the time I get back you either put out that cigarette or get out of the building.'

He looked at her in silence for a while, trying to focus on her face.

'Or what?'

'Or I shall make sure Josh knows about it.'

He lunged towards her but Ros was already striding away towards the barn entrance. She hardly knew where she was going as she ran towards the main buildings in the farmyard.

Perhaps she might find someone, or locate Ben's office so she could use his phone to try Josh's number again.

In and out of doors she went, shouting for help, checking the outbuildings in the hope of finding someone working. Suddenly she heard voices. Running outside, she saw two farm workers who had just come into the yard. As she approached them another man drove into the yard on a tractor.

'Thank goodness I've found someone,' she said. 'Have any of you seen Josh Carlisle?'

They shook their heads.

'I have,' the one just getting down from the tractor said. 'He's down at the water meadows, looking at the cattle,' he said. 'I've just passed 'im.'

'Good. Bessy is in labour and I think she is in some kind of trouble. She has fallen down, but the chain is too tight around her neck and I can't get it loose. Ben's gone to the hospital with Sarah and no-one's around.'

'Chain?' one of the workers said. 'What's she doing on a chain?'

'Shouldn't be on a chain when she's calving,' another said.

'Look,' Ros said, desperate to get help, 'will one of you go and get Josh, quickly?'

'Of course,' the tractor driver replied. 'I'll take my car. Be faster than going down on the ol' tractor again.'

Ros smiled, pleased to have something

moving at last.

'I'm going back to the barn to stay with her.'

'We'll come with you,' one of the other men said, 'in case we can help.'

The three of them headed for the barn and the tractor driver went to fetch Josh. As they walked, Ros glanced at her watch. It had been nearly twenty minutes since she left to look for help, although it seemed much longer. She looked sideways at the men striding out beside her. They were tall and well built. Strength and stamina were going to be an advantage, she acknowledged, especially if there was any chance of getting Bessy out of the chain easily.

They turned a corner and headed towards the barn. One of the men stopped suddenly.

'What is that?' he exclaimed, pointing to the barn.

Her gaze went skywards. Wisps of smoke were puffing through the tiles on the barn roof!

CHAPTER SEVEN

Ros ran after the men, her heart pounding wildly. Inside the barn, flames were licking up the far wall and the air was thick with smoke and the sound of crackling wood. The men, shielding their eyes, ran as far up the barn as they were able, to try and see what they could

100

do to put the fire out.

Ros ran to Bessy. The animal was still in the same position, but now she could see that the front feet and nose of Bessy's calf were visible. Ros turned to the men who had run back to her.

'Quick! Help me get her up so we can find the clasp on the chain and get it off,' she said.

'We'll never manage that,' one said. 'There aren't enough of us here to lift her weight. We'd need the forklift to do that. Besides, we must try to put out the fire first. We are going to move the straw bales out of the barn, get as much straw off the floor as possible. Hopefully we can stop it before it spreads farther. It's a slim chance, and I'm not optimistic, but we'll try.'

As he spoke, there was a whooshing sound behind them as more bales caught fire and flames leaped into the smoke-filled air. Josh ran into the barn at that moment and appeared at Ros's side together with the man who had gone to find him, and Robert. Josh squeezed her shoulder.

'What's the situation, boys?' he shouted.

'Not good, boss,' one said. 'Them bales at the end have caught. We thought we could move them before they went up, but it's too late.'

'Has anyone called the fire brigade?'

'Yes, I have,' Robert said.

'Good. What happened here?' Josh asked.

The men all started talking at once, but when Ros caught Robert's eye he remained silent and avoided her gaze. They weren't able to tell Josh much.

'OK, we'll get to the bottom of this later,' Josh said. 'Let's get organised now. See if we can get the rope around her shoulders and heave her up enough for Ros to get the chain unhooked. It might be possible to drag her out.'

Ros noticed a couple of the men looking at him sceptically. Josh pointed to a couple of workers.

'You men, round the other side. Ros, I want you to get up by her head. Feel around her neck until you can locate the connecting pieces of the chain. One end is a circle. The other end is shaped like a T. The T-piece is fitted through the circle and has to be manoeuvred out of it. Do you understand so far?'

Ros nodded.

'Good. Get up by her head now. We are going to try to rope her. As soon as you feel the pressure ease, try to get the chain off.'

'OK.'

Ros kneeled in the straw at Bessy's head and ran her hands around the animal's neck until she located the join Josh had described. The smoke was making breathing almost impossible and even though she was near the floor, Ros could no longer see the end of the barn. She dragged smoke-laden air into her lungs and coughed, as the men put every ounce of strength they had into trying to lift the now terrified animal.

'Right, lift, now!' Josh shouted.

It was an impossible task, but they tried again and again. Ros was becoming unnerved by the continuing bellowing of the animal, the flames crackling, and the intermittent loud bangs as parts of the barn structure exploded in the savage heat. In the distance she heard a fire engine. Would it be in time? It had to be. She couldn't contemplate the alternative. The men were coughing.

'Wrap your scarf around your face,' Josh shouted.

Ros pulled the long scarf out of her jacket and wound it around her head, covering her nose and mouth and securing the ends inside her jacket. It didn't help her. The smoke was still burning her throat.

She heard Josh say, 'This isn't going to work.'

The air was suddenly filled with a loud noise as part of the roof collapsed at the far end of the barn. Flames leaped towards them and they were engulfed in thick, black smoke.

'Everyone out,' Josh shouted through the smoke. 'Quickly! Now!'

The men ran for the door as if their lives depended on it, stumbling out of the barn coughing loudly and trying to shield their eyes from the smoke. Ros couldn't believe they were leaving, even Josh. She stayed where she was, on her knees at the animal's head. In the distance she heard Josh shouting her name. A second later he shouted from the doorway.

'Ros? Ros? Are you still in there?'

She opened her mouth to call to him, but only succeeded in dragging in more smoke. She bent over, coughing violently. He was at her side in a moment, gripping her shoulders and forcing her to her feet.

'You stupid girl! What are you trying to do? Kill yourself?' he shouted at her. 'You've got to get out of here, now.'

Nearby, Ros saw sparks flash off in all directions and heard the crackling of old wood as the fire raged out of control. Sounds like gunshots split the air as roof tiles cracked under the intense heat. Ros pulled away from him.

'I'm not leaving Bessy,' she shouted back. 'I heard the fire-engine. It's coming, I know it!'

Josh grabbed Ros and started to pull her away.

'No, you don't understand. The animal's frightened. I've got to stay and try to keep her calm until they put out the fire.'

Ros tried to wriggle out of his grip, but his hands around her wrists were like steel. The heifer bellowed again.

'We can't leave her, Josh. She needs us. I'm staying.'

She heard him grunt, just a second before

her feet left the ground and she was swung over his shoulder like a sack of potatoes.

'You're doing no such thing, my lady,' he ground out. 'You're coming with me.'

Out of the burning barn he ran, across the yard and on to the grass verge by the wall where the others were standing, well out of range of the fire. He dumped her unceremoniously on the wet grass. Her scarf slipped off her face and fresh air hit her. She gulped it in greedily.

Josh was half-leaning against the wall, chest heaving, fighting for breath after his exertion. Straw clung to his clothes, his dark hair was awry and his eyes red and watering from the effects of the smoke. Ros absentmindedly put a hand up to her own hair and pulled out a few pieces of straw. The men were standing nearby, talking quietly amongst themselves, worried. Ros noticed Robert standing a little to one side, looking surprisingly sober.

'All accounted for?' Josh asked.

The men all nodded. Ros pulled herself to her feet as two firemen in breathing apparatus ran around the corner of the yard towards the barn. One of them turned and shouted something Ros couldn't hear. Water snaked from the hose and the men carried on towards the barn, aiming the hose at the flames.

Ros began to follow them. She heard a shout and turned around. It was Josh heading after her. She immediately picked up speed and started to run. He was too quick for her and grabbed her before she had gone very far.

'And just where do you think you're going?'

Ros glared at him.

'I've told you,' she said, speaking as though to someone of limited intelligence, 'I'm going to help Bessy.'

She pointed towards the barn.

'See? The firemen are here now. It's going to be OK.'

'Nobody goes near that barn until the firemen give us permission, and that means you, too,' Josh said in an exasperated voice. 'Look, why do you think the firemen aren't going in?'

She looked at the barn and saw that one fireman was playing the water on to the barn and the other had peered into the entrance of the barn and gone round the side of it not into it. She also saw another plume of water coming across the roof as a second hose was trained on the building from the far side.

'But why aren't they going in?' a bewildered Ros asked.

Josh looked deeply into Ros's eyes and spoke quietly.

'Because they think the roof is going to collapse. Rosalin, I have to tell you. There's no chance of saving Bessy.'

'I don't believe you! You're lying,' she shouted at him. 'The fruition of all Tom's work with the herd is in that barn. I can't let that die. Don't you understand?'

She twisted and turned in his arms.

'If Bessy dies it will all have been for nothing. And what about the calf? Surely we can save that?'

She had to get away from him.

'Let go of me,' she shouted hysterically.

'Just listen to me, Ros.'

'No! I won't!'

Josh raised his hand and slapped her across the face, hard. Shocked and stunned, Ros felt tears well up as she stared up at him, eyes wide with pain. Slowly she put her hand to her face, touching the place he hit. Josh's face was anguished. He groaned and pulled her to him, wrapping his arms tightly around. He bent to kiss her smoky hair.

'Ros,' he whispered, 'please, please forgive me. I can't take the risk of you charging off into the barn again. It's too dangerous in there.'

He pushed her away from him gently and stared intently into her eyes.

'Do you honestly think I would leave an animal in a situation like this if there was a chance, no matter how slight, of saving it?'

Ros stared back at him, searching his face for an answer. His eyes were full of honesty and pain and she knew he felt as utterly hopeless as she did. She lowered her eyes and swallowed hard. Someone nearby cleared his throat. Ros and Josh both turned around.

A fireman said, 'Excuse me, sir, but I believe you are in charge here, is that right?'

Josh nodded.

'I wonder if I could have a word, please. It won't take long.'

'Of course.'

The fireman started to walk away and Josh held Ros's hand and started to pull her after him.

'No,' Ros said. 'You go. I'll be fine.'

'If you think I am leaving you out here on your own you must think I'm mad. Look, Robert is over there. If you won't come with me he can stay with you until I get back.'

Ros was too shocked to say anything and allowed Josh to walk her over to where Robert stood, alone, as though carved from stone.

'Robert, would you look after Ros for me, please? I have to go and speak to the fire officer and she won't come with me. Don't leave her on her own and don't under any circumstances let her go near the barn. OK?'

Robert nodded. Josh looked at Ros and smiled.

'I'll be back soon. You won't even know I've gone. Will you wait here? I won't be long.'

Ros nodded.

'Promise?'

A slight pause, then she nodded again. He seemed to accept her answers, such as they were, and hastily followed the fireman across the yard. Ros and Robert eyed each other

108

warily. He opened his mouth to say something.

'Don't say a word,' Ros ground out, shaking from head to foot. 'Don't ever speak to me again.'

Anger and hate rose in her as she thought how this drunken man had been responsible for the whole thing and here he stood, looking as sober as she was.

'Get out of my sight, now, before I do the same to you as you've just done to that defenceless animal.'

Robert's face went white, Ros was pleased to note, and he stepped back from her.

'You heard me. I don't ever want to see you again. Get out of my sight.'

He didn't need to be told twice. He turned on his heels and walked away. Ros stood where she was for a while, at a loss to know what to do with herself. The horror that was being enacted in front of her hadn't yet sunk in and shock was keeping the pain at bay. Suddenly there was a shout. She turned in time to see the firemen running away from the barn. Seconds later the rest of the roof collapsed, sending sparks and flames into the darkening afternoon sky.

She glanced across at the men. They looked defeated, unable to cope with the horror of the situation. They had tried their best, yet it hadn't been good enough. As Ros watched, one of them put his hands in his pockets, lowered his head and slowly walked away.

Ros turned away from the sight of the almost ruined barn, still blazing away, and ran for her life. Sobs racked her body but she took as little notice of them as the tears that streamed down her face, blurring her vision.

CHAPTER EIGHT

It was dark when Rosalind finally returned to the house, and it was ablaze with lights. Even the lanterns on the bridge across the moat were lit up. Near the front door a group of men were listening to someone talking and as Ros drew near she recognised Josh's voice.

'That's the farm completely checked, and her car is still in the garage, so she must be around here somewhere. We'll search the park next. She might be lying out there injured, so spread out like you did before, flashing your torches. You all know the land better than I do, so look in all the hollows you know, just in case she has fallen into one and is injured.'

Ros walked silently over the bridge and she heard the men murmur their agreement.

Dear heavens, Ros thought, startled. They must have been looking for me. She moved forwards, anxious now to tell them she was safe. The crunch of the gravel under her feet was heard by one of the men who turned and noticed her in the gloom.

'Here she is, boss.'

Everyone turned expectantly as Josh strode through the group of men to reach her, wrapping his arms around her as he did so.

'Thank goodness you're back.'

Ros felt relieved to be encircled in his embrace and a feeling of peace washed over her as she laid her head against his waterproof jacket. He put her gently away from him and gave her a long, searching look, then put one arm around her shoulders as the men gathered around, all talking at once.

'We've been worried about you, Ros,' he said. 'Where have you been?'

'I really don't know. That sounds silly, doesn't it? One minute it was daylight, the next thing, it was dark. I got lost, I'm afraid, and only found out where I was about twenty minutes ago. I'm so sorry you have all been put to so much trouble on my account.'

'It's no bother,' one of the men said. 'We're just glad you're safe.'

'You're not hurt, are you?' Josh asked, gripping her shoulder and pulling her closer to him.

'No, I'm fine,' Ros replied, trying to smile. 'I think it must have been the shock. You know, this afternoon.'

She could hardly get the words out, but the men mumbled their acknowledgement of this.

'We understand, miss. Just as long as you are safe.'

This time her smile was genuine.

'Thank you. And thank you all for going to so much trouble for me. I appreciate it.'

Josh thanked the men himself and they moved off, heading back to their own homes, Ros supposed, as she walked slowly to the front door. Catching her up at the door, Josh led her into the light and searched her face again.

'You're sure you feel OK?'

She looked down at her clothes.

'Just wet, dirty and very tired. Josh?'

'Yes?'

'I'm sorry. I feel such a fool for worrying everyone.'

He took her hand.

'Don't apologise, there's no need, Ros. You're safe. That's all that matters.'

They walked into the house together.

'Mrs Barnes, we're home,' Josh shouted.

Mrs Barnes bustled into view and completely took over, fussing over Ros like a hen that had found a lost chicken, shooing her in the direction of a hot bath, some food and bed.

Home—what a wonderful word, Ros thought, as she lay in bed waiting for sleep to claim her. This beautiful house was certainly beginning to feel like home. She pulled herself up sharply. She had to stop thinking that way right now. Josh was probably just being kind to her, and his relatives left a lot to be desired.

She never wanted to see June and Robert again, but they were still Josh's relatives and likely to be around for some time.

When she woke the next morning it was to find sunlight flooding through the bedroom window. Over her feet was an extra eiderdown she recognised as coming from Josh's bed and on top of it was Piglet, the kitten, curled up asleep. She smiled at the contented expression on his little face.

Glancing at her travelling clock on the bedside table she was shocked to see that it was after ten o'clock. Her restless, nightmare-filled night and the previous day made her feel unrested but she knew it would only make matters worse if she lay in bed turning things over in her mind, so she showered and threw on some clothes before heading downstairs. The kitchen was deserted but Mrs Barnes had left a note for her.

Ros—gone shopping, it read. *Breakfast in warming oven in Aga.*

Ros smiled at the thoughtfulness of the housekeeper, but couldn't work up enthusiasm for food, although she did take out a piece of toast. Pouring herself a cup of coffee from the filter, she sat at the scrubbed table and was spreading the toast with some of Mrs Barnes' homemade marmalade when Josh put his head around the door.

'Good, I'm glad you're up and about,' he said, coming into the room. 'Ben's just been down with the good news.'

He sat down beside her looking fresh, as if he had slept well. How could he possibly have managed that after a terrible day like yesterday? Ros supposed it must have been his training as a vet. It wouldn't do to get emotionally involved with the animals or they would never cope with the job.

He smiled and Ros's heart turned over. Her eyes drank in his features, from his dark hair, now in need of a trim, the dark eyes with tawny lights, to the wonderfully mobile mouth that just cried out to be kissed. She knew in that moment that she loved him. The knowledge didn't come as a revelation to her, more a sensation of coming home, of belonging. When had the respect turned to liking, the fondness to love? She didn't know.

What she did know, though, was that there could be no future in it for her. Sadness washed over her. She would have to remember that fact if she were to get through the next week or so until her commission was finished. Rosalind came out of her reverie to find him gazing intently at her. He lifted his brows questioningly.

'A penny for them.'

She shook her head.

'They're not for sale.'

'Oh?'

'Didn't you say there was good news from Ben?'

114

Ros turned the conversation to a safer topic. His look was sceptical, as if he knew what she was doing, but would let it pass.

'Yes, very good news. Sarah had a baby boy in the early hours of this morning and Ben's been going around like a puppy with two tails.'

Ros laughed at Josh's description of his farm manager.

'Oh, that's wonderful, Josh. Is she well?'

'Apparently doing nicely, and the baby, too.'

'Thank heavens something good came out of yesterday.'

Josh took her hand and looked at her seriously for a moment.

'Is it too painful to hear about Bessy?'

Ros shook her head.

'This morning the men dug a grave for her in the small paddock down by the lake. The men from the fire service were here first thing, sifting through the remains of the barn to try to establish the cause of the fire, but now our men will have taken her remains down there and buried her.'

Ros bent her head to hide the tears welling up in her eyes.

'Thank you,' she whispered.

Josh sensed her pain and grief and gripped her hand hard.

'I thought you would like to know, Ros, that we have taken care of her. But it's not the end of Tom's ideas for the herd, you know.'

'No?'

She looked up at him.

'No,' he said, decisively. 'I've decided to continue his work. It may take us some time to reach the stage Tom was at with Bessy, but he's got some good stock in the fields and with a careful breeding programme we can do it, I'm sure.'

'He would have loved that.'

'But would you love it, Ros?'

She looked at him, bemused.

'Why, yes, of course.'

What difference would it make to him to have her approval? In another few days her work would be over and she would be gone. Still, she couldn't help but be glad that Josh was carrying on Tom's plan.

'Good. Now we are on the subject of Tom's ideas I want to tell you that I won't be opening the house to the public, as he wanted to do.'

Ros's heart sank.

'But you still want me to finish the work, don't you?'

Did he now want her to leave right away? She hoped not. Leaving at all was going to be painful enough, without a sudden departure.

'Of course I do. It's just that this house is a wonderful place to bring up children and I wouldn't want them deprived of playing in the rooms and enjoying the old house just so the paying public can wander around. It's not as if I need the money. What do you think?'

'It's up to you, Josh,' she replied, shrugging

her shoulders. 'It would be your property, after all.'

'You wouldn't mind that?'

'It's a wonderful idea.'

Ros tried to keep her smile in place, although the idea of someone else giving Josh the children he so obviously would love filled her with pain.

'Besides, I've a feeling Tom only decided on opening to the public to give him something to do.'

She pushed away her plateful of food. There was no chance of eating even a mouthful of food now.

'If there's nothing else, I must get back to work,' she said, pushing back her chair and standing up.

'Before you go, Ros, I need to ask you about the fire. What exactly happened in the barn yesterday?'

'I think you should ask Robert.'

'I spoke to Ben earlier and he says that Bessy was on a rope yesterday when he gave her to Robert, and he told him to tie her with the rope in the barn.'

'So?'

'There was no need for Bessy to have died. She had what we call obturator nerve paralysis. A nerve was paralysing the back half of her body, so she was unable to deliver the calf herself. That's why she collapsed. We could have saved her if it hadn't been for the fire.'

Rosalind was devastated. Robert certainly had a lot to answer for, one way and another.

'I can't help you, Josh,' she said sadly. 'I wasn't there when the fire started.'

'That's not what I heard.'

'Oh?'

'Robert tells me you went up to see him.'

'I went to see Bessy, not Robert.'

'He also says you distracted him.'

'I what?'

His words startled Ros.

'He says you persuaded him to put his cigarette down for a few moments and he lost track of time.'

Josh's voice was flat.

'You can't be serious!'

Ros's eyes were huge as she came round the table to stand a few feet away from Josh, suddenly realising what he was getting at.

'Are you saying that Robert told you I made a pass at him, is that it?'

'I'm not saying that, Ros, I'm just asking you to tell me what happened.'

'Robert was drunk!' she burst out.

He shot her a surprised look.

'Drunk? He certainly wasn't drunk when I saw him.'

Rosalind sighed. She had the feeling that whatever she said, Josh wouldn't believe her, and who could blame him? Robert sobered up by the time the fire brigade had arrived. It was amazing what a shock to the system could do to a person.

'Then there's no earthly point me bothering to say another word, is there?' she ground on, despair mingled with anger at his attitude towards her. 'As usual, you aren't prepared to believe anyone but your own family.'

'That's not true, Ros.'

'You promised me, Josh, that things would be different in the future, but here you are doubting me yet again.'

She turned towards the door, desperate to get away, but he grabbed her and spun her around to face him.

'Rosalind, for goodness' sake, listen to me.'

'Get away from me, Josh Carlisle. Get away and stay away,' she shouted. 'I've had it with you and your family.'

He made a move towards her but Ros backed to the kitchen door.

'I'm going to finish my commission in the fastest time possible and leave this house, and if I never see you or your relatives again, it won't be too soon for me!'

'Don't do this, Ros. Give me a chance to—'

'Explain?' she cut in. 'Forget it. You've had all the chances you're going to get.'

Ros turned and ran out of the kitchen, along the passage to the stairs and up to the relative safety of her workroom, pain tearing at her heart. How could he do this to her? Could he seriously believe it was her fault the barn burned down, causing Bessy to lose her life? He obviously did, having heard Robert's version of events.

Her pain was too deep for tears and Rosalind stood, dry-eyed, gazing out of the latticed window, her arms tightly wrapped around her, wishing with all her heart that Josh Carlisle had never come into her life.

CHAPTER NINE

Rosalind worked all day with a vengeance, foregoing lunch for an apple and a piece of cheese eaten at her desk. She made a list of the last items to be tackled for the commission, dove-tailing her workload to make the most of every available minute. She decided to work during the evenings, too, hoping to cut valuable hours from her schedule.

Losing track of time, Ros had to be reminded to go down for dinner by Mrs Barnes. The last thing she wanted was to face Josh. Her feelings fluctuated wildly, one minute unable to bear the thought of his company, the next never wanting to be apart from him. She was perversely disappointed to discover that he wouldn't be eating with them as the housekeeper had laid the kitchen table for two. She wondered if he was avoiding her, but this idea was dispelled when Mrs Barnes gave Ros a note from Josh.

'He had to dash out this afternoon and said not to wait for him. He would eat something when he got back,' the housekeeper said.

Ros read the note.

Have some pressing business at the farm, it read, *but would like to see you later this evening.*

Ros sighed. If work was all he wanted to discuss, he was welcome. Just as long as he wasn't going to start on her again about the fire at the barn.

She immersed herself in her work after dinner, squashing thoughts of Josh and their forthcoming meeting, concentrating instead on finishing chores and ticking them off her list. She finished hand-sewing the hems on a pair of curtains for one of the bedrooms and took them along to hang. Another room completed, she thought, as she stood back to admire her handiwork. Ros had to admit the room looked good. Then she heard a voice behind her.

'That looks really great, Ros. You have a wonderful eye for detail.'

She turned around to see Josh leaning nonchalantly on the door frame, admiring the view.

'Is this room finished now?'

Pleased with his praise, she nodded.

'Only one more to do.'

'Good, then you can stop for the evening. Yes?'

'Well, yes, I suppose so.'

'Then let's go. I've got something to show you.'

'Oh? What?'

'You'll have to come and see, won't you?'

She followed him reluctantly. Sport they had collected coats, crossed the moat and headed for the garage where Josh reversed out the Land-Rover and opened the front passenger door for her.

'Where are we going?'

Ros was beginning to get concerned. There was a definite change in Josh's treatment of her, a kind of no-nonsense attitude with a touch of stubbornness thrown in.

'Not far. Hop in, and we'll be off. It won't take long, and put on your seat belt.'

She climbed into the vehicle reluctantly and they set off, skirting the moat as though going up the back lane to the farm. But as soon as he got on to the lane, he swung off right and drove the vehicle straight at the hedge. Ros gave a shriek of fright as the vehicle plunged through the hedge, paintwork scraping, side mirrors flattening against windows. Ros heard a loud cracking sound and feared for the state of the bumper.

'Are you totally insane?' she shouted at him, as he drove right across beds of rose bushes in the formal garden and straight towards the lake.

The vehicle ate up the ground as comfortably as if it was running on a normal road. Bushes were flattened and ripped from the ground and areas of lawn were churned up into furrows as the vehicle ploughed on. Josh turned briefly and smiled at her.

'No, Ros, I think I'm finally getting sane.'

'But whatever are you doing this for? I thought you wanted to show me something?'

He nodded.

'And what, exactly, do you want to show me?'

The headlights picked up the silver glitter of the ornamental lake racing towards them in the dark.

'The lake, Josh. For goodness' sake, we're heading straight for it.'

'Of course. That's what I want to show you. The lake.'

'But, Josh, we could have walked over the little, wooden bridge from the lawn. Why do this? Think about the hedge, the bushes, the garden—the car, even.'

'They can get fixed. Something else may never get fixed unless we sort it out tonight. Besides, would you have come?'

Ros could answer that truthfully. She didn't pretend to understand him, but wasn't about to argue. Josh drove the vehicle into the lake, a huge plume of water rising over the bonnet and windscreen. Ros ducked, and immediately felt silly. At least it was dry inside. He drove steadily on until they were roughly in the middle of the lake, stopped, turned off the ignition and put the keys in his pocket. Water lapped and sucked at the vehicle and eventually became calm. Neither Ros nor Josh spoke. The headlights shone out over the placid water in the silence. Eventually Ros cleared her throat.

'Do you want to tell me what this is about?'

'Yes. I want to talk to you without you running off in a huff all the time and taking things the wrong way.'

'I don't.'

'Yes, you do.'

'No, I don't!'

He sighed in exasperation.

'Ros. Shut up and listen. I want you to hear me out, and I can't get you to listen to me. I thought if I brought you here you might stay put long enough for me to have my say.'

'Wonderful. I can't leave even if I wanted to.'

'Yes, you can. The doors aren't locked. The water is only about a foot deep. You can wade to the bank and be off whenever you want and only get your feet wet.'

Ros threw him a mutinous look. She knew that the man-made lake's bottom consisted of large, smooth stones. If she tried to walk on them, covered in slime as they were sure to be, she would get a lot more than her feet wet, as well he knew.

'Then talk.'

She could feel him smiling in the darkness.

'Right. Well, then, you'll have noticed that I have been very busy today. I've been organising the removal of Robert and June from the farm.'

Ros was so shocked she couldn't say a word.

'Cat got your tongue?' he asked.

Ros nodded then managed, 'But why?'

'For the same reasons I was trying to tell you this morning, which you refused to listen to.'

Ros had the feeling she was going to look a real idiot, and that moment wasn't too far away.

'What I was so busy trying to tell you this morning was that when the fire brigade people came to inspect the scene this morning they found small fragments of glass in the ruin of the barn. They said tests could be done, but they reckoned they came from a bottle, an alcohol bottle. Forensics are so good these days they'll probably be able to tell us what had been in the bottle.'

'Oh.'

She was unhappy for Josh. How must it feel to know that your brother was an alcoholic and had destroyed so much that was precious by his addiction?

'I'm sorry.'

'So am I Ros, desperately sorry, for Robert, for Bessy, for the whole sordid mess. It stood out a mile that Robert must have been responsible for the barn burning down. I had already confronted him before I came down to see you and he broke down. I think the shock of what actually happened hit him hard. He must have sobered up when he realised things were getting out of control and he went to ring the fire brigade.'

'But why would he do a thing like that?'

'Who knows why people do the things they do, Ros, but at least he and June are out of my hair at last. I've promised him that I won't prosecute, providing he stays away. I've also offered some money if he will go and get treatment, but whether he will, or not, is anybody's guess.'

'So you believed what I said this morning?'

'Of course. There wasn't any doubt in my mind. I just wanted to hear about it from your side, so I could piece together exactly what led up to it.'

Ros felt her face burn with embarrassment.

'But I wouldn't let you say it. I just got on my high horse again and cantered off into the distance.'

Josh laughed.

'I suppose I'll have to get used to it,' he replied, trying to sound martyred.

Ros sat still, hardly able to speak.

'Why?' she said eventually.

Josh leaned towards Ros.

'Come here.'

She met him halfway. He drew her close and kissed her, making her whole body tingle.

'Because I love you, Rosalind. Haven't you guessed?'

'June says you can't love anybody,' Ros said.

'Really? So you believe her, do you?'

'No. Well, not really.'

She crossed her fingers and hoped she would be forgiven for even listening to what the other woman had said. He raked a hand through his hair.

'I knew June years ago, before Robert did. We used to go out for a while, until I discovered what sort of person she really was. Then I dropped her. End of story. She met Robert through me. But I don't want to discuss them. Ros, I want to marry you, and I know you feel the same about me.'

'Do you indeed?'

Ros was suddenly feeling a lot happier.

'Want to deny it?'

Ros shook her head.

'Good.'

He pulled her closer.

'Marry me, Ros, and I'll try to keep you off high horses.'

A smile lit up her face as she held him close, oblivious to the little convoy of vehicles, including the tractor, heading through the gap in the hedge towards the lake.

'Sounds like a good idea to me. I'd already decided to give up horses for Highland cattle, anyway.'

Josh smiled at her and, as he lowered his

mouth to hers and kissed her with tenderness and passion, Rosalind knew she had finally come home.

We hope you have enjoyed this Large
Print book. Other Chivers Press or
Thorndike Press Large Print books are
available at your library or directly from the
publishers.

For more information about current and
forthcoming titles, please call or write,
without obligation, to:

Chivers Press Limited
Windsor Bridge Road
Bath BA2 3AX
England
Tel. (01225) 335336

OR

G.K. Hall & Co.
295 Kennedy Memorial Drive
Waterville
Maine 04901
USA

All our Large Print titles are designed for
easy reading, and all our books are made to
last.